Torquato Tasso, Dante Alighieri, Leigh Hunt, Lodovico Ariosto

Stories from the Italian Poets

with critical notices of the life and genius of the authors - Vol. 2

Torquato Tasso, Dante Alighieri, Leigh Hunt, Lodovico Ariosto

Stories from the Italian Poets
with critical notices of the life and genius of the authors - Vol. 2

ISBN/EAN: 9783337602642

Printed in Europe, USA, Canada, Australia, Japan

Cover: Foto ©Andreas Hilbeck / pixelio.de

More available books at **www.hansebooks.com**

STORIES

FROM

THE ITALIAN POETS

(SECOND SERIES)

BERNARDO TASSO

AND

LUDOVICO GIOVANNI ARIOSTO

WITH CRITICAL NOTICES OF THE LIVES AND
GENIUS OF THE AUTHORS

BY

LEIGH HUNT

NEW YORK AND LONDON

G. P. PUTNAM'S SONS

The Knickerbocker Press

CONTENTS

TASSO

TASSO :

CRITICAL NOTICE OF HIS LIFE AND GENIUS.

CRITICAL NOTICE OF TASSO'S LIFE AND GENIUS.*

THE romantic poetry of Italy having risen to its highest and apparently its most lawless pitch in the "Orlando Furioso," a reaction took place in the next age in the "Jerusalem Delivered." It did not hurt, however, the popularity of Ariosto. It only increased the number of poetic readers ; and under the auspices, or rather the control, of a Luther-fearing church,

* My authorities for this notice are, Black's "Life of Tasso" (2 vols. 4to, 1810), his original, Serassi, "Vita di Torquato Tasso" (do. 1790), and the works of the poet in the Pisan edition of Professor Rosini (33 vols. 8vo, 1832). I have been indebted to nothing in Black which I have not ascertained by reference to the Italian biographer, and quoted nothing stated by Tasso himself but from the works. Black's Life, which is a free version of Serassi's, modified by the translator's own opinions and criticism, is elegant, industrious, and interesting. Serassi's was the first copious biography of the poet founded on original documents ; and it deserved to be translated by Mr. Black, though servile to the house of Este, and, as might be expected, far from being always ingenious. Among other instances of this writer's want of candor is the fact of his having been the discoverer and suppresser of the manuscript review of Tasso by Galileo. The best

produced, if not as classical a work as it claimed
to be, or one, in the true sense of the word, as
catholic as its predecessor, yet certainly a far
more Roman Catholic and at the same time
very delightful fiction.   The circle of fabulous
narrative was thus completed, and a link formed,
though in a very gentle and qualified manner,
both with Dante's theocracy and the obvious
regularity of the "Æneid," the oldest romance
of Italy.

The author of this epic of the Crusades was of
a family so noble and so widely diffused, that,
under the patronage of the emperors and the
Italian princes, it flourished in a very remarkable manner, not only in its own country, but
in Flanders, Germany, and Spain.   There was a
Tasso once in England, ambassador of Philip
the Second; another, like Cervantes, distin-

summary account of the poet's life and writings which I
have met with is Ginguéné's, in the fifth volume of his
"Histoire Littéraire," etc.   It is written with his usual
grace, vivacity, and acuteness, and contains a good notice of the Tasso controversy.   As to the Pisan edition of
the works, it is the completest, I believe, in point of con-
tents, ever published, comprises all the controversial
criticism, and is, of course, very useful ; but it contains
no life except Manso's (now known to be very inconclu-
sive), has got a heap of feeble variorum comments on
the "Jerusalem," no notes worth speaking of to the rest
of the works, and, notwithstanding the claim in the title-
page to the merit of a "better order," has left the correspondence in a deplorable state of irregularity, as well
as totally without elucidation.   The learned Professor is
an agreeable writer, and I believe a very pleasant man,
but he certainly is a provoking editor.

guished himself at the battle of Lepanto ; and
a third gave rise to the sovereign German house
of Tour and Taxis. *Taxus* is the Latin of Tasso.
The Latin word, like the Italian, means both a
badger and a yew-tree ; and the family in general appear to have taken it in the former sense.
The animal is in their coat-of-arms. But the
poet, or his immediate relatives, preferred being more romantically shadowed forth by the
yew-tree. The parent stock of the race was at
Bergamo in Lombardy ; and here was born the
father of Tasso, himself a poet of celebrity,
though his fame has been eclipsed by that of
his son.

Bernardo Tasso, author of many elegant
lyrics, of some volumes of letters, not uninteresting but too florid, and of the "Amadigi,"
an epic romance now little read, was a man of
small property, very honest and good-hearted,
but restless, ambitious, and with a turn for expense beyond his means. He attached himself
to various princes, with little ultimate advantage, particularly to the unfortunate Sanseverino, Prince of Salerno, whom he faithfully
served for many years. The prince had a high
sense of his worth, and would probably have
settled him in the wealth and honors he
was qualified to adorn, but for those Spanish
oppressions in the history of Naples which

ended in the ruin of both master and servant.
Bernardo, however, had one happy interval
of prosperity; and during this, at the age of
forty-six, he married Porzia di Rossi, a young
lady of a rich and noble family, with a claim to
a handsome dowry. He spent some delightful
years with her at Sorrento, a spot so charming
as to have been considered the habitation of the
Sirens; and here, in the midst of his orange-
trees, his verses, and the breezes of an aromatic
coast, he had three children, the eldest of whom
was a daughter named Cornelia, and the youngest the author of the "Jerusalem Delivered."
The other child died young. The house distinguished by the poet's birth was restored from
a dilapidated condition by order of Joseph Bona-
parte when King of Naples, and is now a hotel.

Torquato Tasso was born March 11, 1544,
nine years after the death of Ariosto, who was
intimate with his father. He was very devoutly
brought up, and grew so tall and became so
premature a scholar, that at nine, he tells
us, he might have been taken for a boy
of twelve. At eleven, in consequence of the
misfortunes of his father, who had been exiled
with the Prince of Salerno, he was forced to
part from his mother, who remained at home
to look after a dowry which she never received.
Her brothers deprived her of it; and in two

years' time she died—Bernardo thought by poison. Twenty-four years afterwards her illustrious son, in the midst of his own misfortunes, remembered with sighs the tears with which the kisses of his poor mother were bathed when she was forced to let him go.*

The little Torquato following, as he says, like another Ascanius, the footsteps of his wandering father, joined Bernardo in Rome. After two years' study in that city, partly under an old priest who lived with them, the vicissitudes of the father's lot took away the son first to Bergamo, among his relations, and then to

---

* In the beautiful fragment beginning, "O del grand' Apennino":

"Me dal sen della madre empia fortuna
   Pargoletto divelse. Ah! di que' baci,
 Ch' ella bagnò di lagrime dolenti,
 Con sospir mi rimembra, e degli ardenti
 Preghi, che sen portár l' aure fugaci,
 Ch' io giunger non dovea più volto a volto
 Fra quelle braccia accalto
 Con nodi così stretti e sì tenaci.
 Lasso! e seguii con mal sicure piante,
 Qual Ascanio, o Camilla, il padre errante."

Me from my mother's bosom my hard lot
Took when a child. Alas! though all these years
I have been used to sorrow,
I sigh to think upon the floods of tears
Which bathed her kisses on that doleful morrow:
I sigh to think of all the prayers and cries
She wasted, straining me with lifted eyes:
For never more on one another's face
Was it our lot to gaze and to embrace!
Her little stumbling boy,
Like to the child of Troy,
Or like to one doomed to no haven rather,
Followed the footsteps of his wandering father.

Pesaro, in the duchy of Urbino, where his education was associated for nearly two years with that of the young prince, afterwards Duke Francesco Maria the Second (della Rovere), who retained a regard for him through life. In 1559 the boy joined his father in Venice, where the latter had been appointed secretary to the Academy; but next year he was withdrawn from these pleasing varieties of scene by the parental delusion so common in the history of men of letters—the study of the law; which Bernardo intended him to pursue henceforth in the city of Padua. He accordingly arrived in Padua at the age of sixteen and a half, and fulfilled his legal destiny by writing the poem of "Rinaldo," which was published in the course of less than two years at Venice. The good-natured and poetic father, convinced by this specimen of jurisprudence how useless it was to thwart the hereditary passion, permitted him to devote himself wholly to literature, which he therefore went to study in the university of Bologna; and there, at the early age of nineteen, he began his "Jerusalem Delivered"; that is to say, he planned it, and wrote three cantos, several of the stanzas of which he retained when the poem was matured. He quitted Bologna, however, in a fit of indignation at being accused of the authorship of a satire; and after visiting some friends at Castelvetro and Correggio, returned to Padua on the invitation of his friend Scipio Gonzaga, afterwards cardinal, who wished him to become a member of an academy he had instituted, called the *Eterei* (Ethereals). Here he studied his favorite philosopher, Plato, and composed three Discourses on Heroic Poetry, dedicated to his friend. He now paid a visit to his father in Mantua, where the unsettled man had become secretary to the duke ; and here, it is said, he fell in love with a young lady of a distinguished family, whose name was Laura Peperara ; but this did not hinder him from returning to his Paduan studies, in which he spent nearly the whole of the following year. He was then informed that the Cardinal of Este, to whom he had dedicated his "Rinaldo," and with whom interest had been made for the purpose, had appointed him one of his attendants, and that he was expected at Ferrara by the 1st of December. Returning to Mantua, in order to prepare for this appointment with his father, he was seized with a dangerous illness, which detained him there nearly a twelvemonth longer. On his recovery he hastened to Ferrara, and arrived in that city on the last day of October, 1565, the first of many years of glory and misery.

The Cardinal of Este was the brother of the

reigning Duke of Ferrara, Alfonso the Second,
grandson of the Alfonso of Ariosto. It is curious to see the two most celebrated romantic
poets of Italy thrown into unfortunate connection with two princes of the same house and
the same respective ranks. Tasso's cardinal,
however, though the poet lost his favor, and
though very little is known about him, left no
such bad reputation behind him as Ippolito. It
was in the service of the duke that the poet experienced his sufferings.

This prince, who was haughty, ostentatious,
and quarrelsome, was, at the time of the stranger's arrival, rehearsing the shows and tourna-
ments intended to welcome his bride, the sister
of the Emperor Maximilian the Second. She
was his second wife. The first was a daughter
of the rival house of Tuscany, which he detested;
and the marriage had not been happy. The
new consort arrived in the course of a few
weeks, entering the city in great pomp; and
for a time all went happily with the young
poet. He was in a state of ecstacy with the
beauty and grandeur he beheld around him—
obtained the favorable notice of the duke's two
sisters and the duke himself—went on with
his "Jerusalem Delivered," which, in spite of
the presence of Ariosto's memory, he was resolved to load with praises of the house of Este;

and in this tumult of pride and expectation, he beheld the duke, like one of the heroes of his poem, set out to assist the emperor against the Turks at the head of three hundred gentlemen, armed at all points, and mantled in various colored velvets embroidered with gold.

To complete the young poet's happiness, or commence his disappointments, he fell in love, notwithstanding the goddess he had left in Mantua, with the beautiful Lucrezia Bendidio, who does not seem, however, to have loved in return; for she became the wife of a Macchiavelli. Among his rivals was Guarini, who afterwards emulated him in pastoral poetry, and who accused him on this occasion of courting two ladies at once.

Guarini's accusation has been supposed to refer to the duke's sister Leonora, whose name has become so romantically mixed up with the poet's biography; but the latest inquiries render it probable that the allusion was to Laura Peperara.* The young poet, however, who had not escaped the influence of the free manners of Italy, and whose senses and vanity may hitherto have been more interested than his heart, rhymed and flattered on all sides of him, not of course omitting the charms of princesses. In

* Rosini, "Saggio sugli Amori di Torquato Tasso," etc., in the Professor's edition of his works, vol. xxxiii.

order to win the admiration of the ladies in a body, he sustained for three days, in public, after the fashion of the times, "Fifty Amorous Conclusions"; that is to say, affirmations on the subject of love; doubtless to the equal delight of his fair auditors and himself, and the creation of a good deal of jealousy and ill-will on the part of such persons of his own sex as had not wit or spirits enough for the display of so much logic and love-making.

In 1569, the death of his father, who had been made governor of Ostiglia by the Duke of Mantua, cost the loving son a fit of illness; but the continuation of his "Jerusalem," an "Oration" spoken at the opening of the Ferrarese academy, the marriage of Leonora's sister Lucrezia with the Prince of Urbino, and the society of Leonora herself, who led the retired life of a person in delicate health, and was fond of the company of men of letters, helped to divert him from melancholy recollections; and a journey to France, at the close of the year following, took him into scenes that were not only totally new, but otherwise highly interesting to the singer of Godfrey of Boulogne. The occasion of it was a visit of the cardinal, his master, to the court of his relative Charles the Ninth. It is supposed that his eminence went to confer with the king on matters relative to the disputes which not long afterwards occasioned the detestable massacre of St. Bartholomew.

Before his departure, Tasso put into the hands of one of his friends a document, which, as it is very curious, and serves to illustrate perhaps more than one cause of his misfortunes, is here given entire.

MEMORIAL LEFT BY TASSO ON HIS DEPARTURE TO FRANCE.

"Since life is frail, and it may please Almighty God to dispose of me otherwise in this my journey to France, it is requested of Signor Ercole Rondinelli that he will, in that case, undertake the management of the following concerns :

"In the first place, with regard to my compositions, it is my wish that all my love-sonnets and madrigals should be collected and published ; but with regard to those, whether amatory or otherwise, *which I have written for any friend*, my request is, that *they should be buried with myself*, save only the one commencing ' *Or che l' aura mia dolce altrove spira.*' I wish the publication of the ' Oration ' spoken in Ferrara at the opening of the academy, of the four books on ' Heroic Poetry,' of the six last cantos of the ' Godfrey ' (the ' Jerusalem '), and of those stanzas of the two first which shall seem least imperfect. All these compositions, however, are to be submitted to the review and consideration of Signor Scipio Gonzaga, of Signor Domenico Veniero, and of Signor Battista Guarini, who, I persuade myself, will not refuse this trouble, when they consider the zealous friendship I have entertained for themselves.

"Let them be informed, too, that it was my intention that they should cut and hew without mercy whatever should appear to them defective or superfluous. With regard to additions or changes, I should wish them to proceed more cautiously, since, after all, the poem would remain imperfect. As to my other compositions, should there be any which, to the aforesaid Signor Rondinelli and the other gentlemen, might seem not unworthy of publication, let them be disposed of according to their pleasure.

"In respect to my property, I wish that such part of it as I have *pledged to Abram* —— for twenty-five lire, and seven pieces of arras, which are *likewise in pledge to Signor Ascanio for thirteen scudi*, together with whatever I have in this house, should be sold, and that the overplus of the proceeds should go to defray the expense of the following epitaph to be inscribed on a monument to my father, whose body is in St. Polo. And should any impediment take place in these matters, I entreat Signor Ercole

*to have recourse to the favor of the most ex-
cellent Madame Leonora, whose liberality I
confide in, for my sake.*

"I, Torquato Tasso, have written this, Ferrara, 1570."

I shall have occasion to recur to this document
by and by. I will merely observe, for the present, that the marks in it, both of imprudence
in money-matters and confidence in the good-
will of a princess, are very striking. "Abram"
and "Signor Ascanio" were both Jews. The
pieces of arras belonged to his father; and
probably this was an additional reason why the
affectionate son wished the proceeds to defray
the expense of the epitaph. The epitaph recorded his father's poetry, state-services, and
vicissitudes of fortune.

Tasso was introduced to the French king as
the poet of a French hero and of a Catholic
victory; and his reception was so favorable
(particularly as the wretched Charles, the vic-
tim of his mother's bigotry, had himself no
mean poetic feeling), that, with a rash mixture
of simplicity and self-reliance (respect makes
me unwilling to call it self-importance), the
poet expressed an impolitic amount of astonishment at the favor shown at court to the
Hugonots—little suspecting the horrible de-

sign it covered. He shortly afterwards broke with his master the cardinal; and it is supposed that this unseasonable escape of zeal was the cause. He himself appears to have thought so.*

Perhaps the cardinal only wanted to get the imprudent poet back to Italy; for, on Tasso's return to Ferrara, he was not only received into the service of the duke with a salary of some fifteen golden scudi a month, but told that he was exempted from any particular duty, and might attend in peace to his studies. Balzac affirms, that while Tasso was at the court of France, he was so poor as to beg a crown from a friend; and that, when he left it, he had the same coat on his back that he came in.† The assertions of a professed wit and hyperbolist are not to be taken for granted; yet it is difficult to say to what shifts improvidence may not be reduced.

The singer of the house of Este would now, it might have been supposed, be happy. He had leisure; he had money; he had the worldly honors that he was fond of; he occupied himself in perfecting the "Jerusalem"; and he wrote his beautiful pastoral, the "Aminta," which was performed before the duke and his

---

* "Lettere Inedite," p. 33, in the "Opere," vol. xvii.

† "Entretiens," 1663, p. 169, quoted by Serassi, pp. 175, 182.

court to the delight of the brilliant assembly.
The duke's sister Lucrezia, Princess of Urbino,
who was a special friend of the poet, sent for
him to read it to her at Pesaro ; and in course
of the ensuing carnival it was performed with
similar applause at the court of her father-in-
law. The poet had been as much enchanted by
the spectacle which the audience at Ferrara
presented to his eyes, as the audience with the
loves and graces with which he enriched their
stage. The shepherd Thyrsis, by whom he
meant himself, reflected it back upon them in
a passage of the performance. It is worth while
dwelling on this passage a little, because it
exhibits a brief interval of happiness in the
author's life, and also shows us what he had
already begun to think of courts at the moment
he was praising them. But he ingeniously con-
trives to put the praise in his own mouth, and
the blame in another's. The shepherd's friend,
Mopsus (by whom Tasso is thought to have
meant Speroni), had warned him against going
to court :

> " Però, figlio,
> Va su l' avviso," etc.

" Therefore, my son, take my advice. Avoid
The places where thou seest much drapery,
Colors, and gold, and plumes, and heraldries,
And such new-fanglements. But, above all,
Take care how evil chance or youthful wandering

Bring thee upon the house of Idle Babble."
"What place is that?" said I ; and he resumed :—
"Enchantresses dwell there, who make one see
Things as they are not, ay and hear them too.
That which shall seem pure diamond and fine gold
Is glass and brass ; and coffers that look silver,
Heavy with wealth, are baskets full of bladders.*
The very walls there are so strangely made,
They answer those who talk ; and not in syllables,
Or bits of words, like echo in our woods,
But go the whole talk over, word for word,
With something else besides, that no one said.†
The tressels, tables, bedsteads, curtains, lockers,
Chairs, and whatever furniture there is
In room or bedroom, all have tongues and speech,
And are for ever tattling. Idle Babble
Is always going about, playing the child ;
And should a dumb man enter in that place,
The dumb would babble in his own despite.
And yet this evil is the least of all
That might assail thee. Thou might'st be arrested
In fearful transformation to a willow,
A beast, fire, water,—fire for ever sighing,
Water for ever weeping."—Here he ceased :
And I, with all this fine foreknowledge, went
To the great city ; and, by Heaven's kind will,
Came where they live so happily. The first sound
I heard was a delightful harmony,
Which issued forth, of voices loud and sweet ;—
Sirens, and swans, and nymphs, a heavenly noise
Of heavenly things ;—which gave me such delight,
That, all admiring, and amazed, and joyed,

---

* Suggested by Ariosto's furniture in the Moon.
† This was a trick which he afterwards thought he had
reason to complain of in a style very different from
pleasantry.

I stopped awhile quite motionless.   There stood
Within the entrance, as if keeping guard
Of those fine things, one of a high-souled aspect,
Stalwart withal, of whom I was in doubt
Whether to think him better knight or leader.*
He, with a look at once benign and grave,
In royal guise, invited me within ;
He, great and in esteem ; me, lorn and lowly.
Oh, the sensations and the sights which then
Shower'd on me.   Goddesses I saw, and nymphs
Graceful and beautiful, and harpers fine
As Linus or as Orpheus ; and more deities,
All without veil or cloud, bright as the virgin
Aurora, when she glads immortal eyes,
And sows her beams and dew drops, silver and gold.

In the summer of 1574, the Duke of Ferrara
went to Venice to pay his respects to the successor of Charles the Ninth, Henry the Third,
then on his way to France from his kingdom
of Poland.   Tasso went with the Duke, and is
understood to have taken the opportunity of
looking for a printer of his "Jerusalem," which
was now almost finished.   Writers were anxious
to publish in that crafty city, because its government would give no security of profit to
books printed elsewhere.   Alfonso, who was in
mourning for Henry's brother, and to whom

‡ Alfonso. The word for " leader " in the original, *duce*,
made the allusion more obvious.   The epithet "royal,"
in the next sentence, conveyed a welcome intimation to
the ducal ear, the house of Este being very proud of its
connection with the sovereigns of Europe, and very desirous of becoming royal itself.

mourning itself only suggested a new occasion of pomp and vanity, took with him to this interview five hundred Ferrarese gentlemen, all dressed in long black cloaks ; who walked about Venice (says a reporter) "by twos and threes," wonderfully impressed the inhabitants with their " gravity and magnificence." * The mourners feasted, however; and Tasso had a quartan fever, which delayed the completion of the "Jerusalem," till next year. This was at length effected ; and now once more, it might have been thought, the writer would have reposed on his laurels.

But Tasso had already begun to experience the uneasiness attending superiority ; and, unfortunately, the strength of his mind was not equal to that of his genius. He was of an ultra-sensitive temperament, and subject to depressing fits of sickness. He could not calmly bear envy. Sarcasm exasperated, and hostile criticism afflicted him. The seeds of a suspicious temper were nourished by prosperity itself. The author of the " Aminta " and the "Jerusalem " began to think the attentions he received unequal to his merits; while with a sort of hysterical mixture of demand for applause, and provocation of censure, he not only condescended to read his poems in manuscript wherever he

* Serassi, vol. i., p. 210.

went, but, in order to secure the good-will of the papal licenser, he transmitted it for revisal to Rome, where it was mercilessly criticized for the space of two years by the bigots and hypocrites of a court, which Luther had rendered a very different one from that in the time of Ariosto.

This new source of chagrin exasperated the complexional restlessness which now made our author think that he should be more easy anywhere than in Ferrara; perhaps more able to communicate with and convince his critics; and, unfortunately, he permitted himself to descend to a weakness the most fatal of all others to a mind naturally exalted and ingenuous. Perhaps it was one of the main causes of all which he suffered. Indeed, he himself, attributed his misfortunes to irresolution. What I mean in the present instance was, that he did not disdain to adopt underhand measures. He showed a face of satisfaction with Alfonso, at the moment that he was taking steps to exchange his court for another. He wrote for that purpose to his friend Scipio Gonzaga, now a prelate at the court of Rome, earnestly begging him, at the same time, not to commit him in their correspondence; and Scipio, who was one of his kindest and most indulgent friends, and who doubtless saw that the Duke of Ferrara and his poet were not of dispositions likely to accord, did all he could to procure him an appointment with one of the family of the Medici.

Most unhappily for this speculation (and perhaps even the good-natured Gonzaga took a little more pleasure in it on that account), Alfonso inherited all the detestation of his house for that lucky race ; and it is remarkable, that the same jealousies which hindered Ariosto's advancement with the Medici were still more fatal to the hopes of Tasso ; for they served to plunge him into the deepest adversity. In vain he had warnings given him, both friendly and hostile. The princess, now Duchess of Urbino, who was his particular friend, strongly cautioned him against the temptation of going away. She said he was watched. He himself thought his letters were opened ; and probably they were. They certainly were at a subsequent period. Tasso, however, persisted, and went to Rome. Scipio Gonzaga introduced him to Cardinal Ferdinand de' Medici, afterwards Grand Duke of Tuscany ; and Ferdinand made him offers of protection so handsome, that they excited his suspicion. The self-tormenting poet thought they savored more of hatred to the Este family, than honor to himself.*

* "Alla lor magnanimità è convenevole il mostrar, ch' amor delle virtù, non odio verso altri, gli abbia già mossi ad invitarmi con invito così largo."—" Opere," vol. xv., p. 94.

He did not accept them. He did nothing
at Rome but make friends, in order to per-
plex them; listen to his critics, in order to
worry himself; and perform acts of piety in the
churches, by way of showing that the love-
scenes in the "Jerusalem" were innocent. For
the bigots had begun to find something very
questionable in mixing up so much love with
war. The bloodshed they had no objection to.
The love bearded their prejudices, and excited
their envy.

Tasso returned to Ferrara, and endeavored
to solace himself with eulogizing two fair
strangers who had arrived at Alfonso's court,—
Eleonora Sanvitale, who had been newly married to the Count of Scandiano (a Tiene, not a
Boiardo, whose line was extinct), and Barbara
Sanseverino, Countess of Sala, her mother-in-
law. The mother-in-law, who was a Juno-like
beauty, wore her hair in the form of a crown.
The still more beautiful daughter-in-law had
an under-lip such as Anacreon or Sir John
Suckling would have admired,—pouting and
provoking,—$\pi\rho\kappa\alpha\lambda\upsilon\mu\epsilon\nu\upsilon\nu$ $\varphi\iota\lambda\eta\mu\alpha$. Tasso
wrote verses on them both, but particularly to
the lip; and this Countess of Scandiano is the
second, out of the three Leonoras, with whom
Tasso was said by his friend Manso to have
been in love. The third, it is now ascertained,
never existed; and his love-making to the new

or second Leonora, goes to show how little of real passion there was in the praises of the first (the Princess Leonora), or probably of any lady at court. He had professed love, as a forlorn hope, to the countess' waiting-maid. Yet these gallantries of sonnets are exalted into bewilderments of the heart.

His restlessness returning, the poet now condescended to craft a second time. Expecting to meet with a refusal, and so be afforded a pretext for quitting Ferrara, he applied for the vacant office of historiographer. It was granted him ; and he then disgusted the Medici by pleading an unlooked-for engagement, which he could only reconcile to his applications for their favor by renouncing his claim to be believed. If he could have deceived others, why might he not have deceived them ?

All the lurking weakness of the poet's temperament began to display itself at this juncture. His perplexity excited him to a degree of irritability bordering on delirium ; and the circumstances conspired to increase it. He had lent an acquaintance the key of his rooms at court, for the purpose (he tells us) of accommodating some intrigue ; and he suspected this person of opening cabinets containing his papers. Remonstrating with him one day in the court of the palace, either on that or some other account, the man gave him the lie. He received in return a blow on the face, and is said by Tasso to have brought a set of his kinsmen to assassinate him, all of whom the heroical poet immediately put to flight. At one time he suspected the duke of jealousy respecting the dedication of his poem, and of another, of a wish to burn it. He suspected his servants. He became suspicious of the truth of his friend Gonzaga. He doubted, even, whether some of the praises addressed to him by Orazio Ariosto, the nephew of the great poet, which, one would have thought, would have been to him a consummation of bliss, were not intended to mystify and hurt him. At length he fancied that his persecutors had accused him of heresy to the Inquisition ; and, as he had gone through the metaphysical doubts, common with most men of reflection respecting points of faith and the mysteries of creation, he feared that some indiscreet words had escaped him, giving color to the charge. He thus beheld enemies all around him. He dreaded stabbing and poison; and one day, in some paroxysm of rage or horror, how occasioned it is not known, ran with a knife or dagger at one of the servants of the Duchess of Urbino in her own chamber.

Alfonso, upon this, apparently in the mildest and most reasonable manner, directed that he should be confined to his apartments, and put into the hands of the physician. These unfortunate events took place in the summer of 1577, and in the poet's thirty-third year.

Tasso showed so much affliction at this treatment, and, at the same time, bore it so patiently, that the duke took him to his beautiful country-seat of Belriguardo; where, in one of his accounts of the matter, the poet says he treated him as a brother; but, in another, he accuses him of having taken pains to make him criminate himself, and confess certain matters, real or supposed, the nature of which is a puzzle to posterity. Some are of opinion (and this is the prevailing one), that he was found guilty of being in love with the Princess Leonora, perhaps of being loved by herself. Others think the love out of the question, and that the duke was concerned in nothing but his endeavoring to transfer his services and his poetic reputation into the hands of the Medici. Others see in the duke's conduct nothing but that of a good master interesting himself in the welfare of an afflicted servant.

It is certain that Alfonso did all he could to prevent the surreptitious printing of the "Jerusalem Delivered" in various towns of Italy, the dread of which had much afflicted the poet ; and he also endeavored, though in vain, to ease his mind on the subject of the Inquisition ; for these facts are attested by state-papers and other documents, not dependent either on the testimony of third persons or the partial representations of the sufferer. But Tasso felt so uneasy at Belriguardo, that he requested leave to retire awhile into a convent. He remained there several days, apparently so much to his satisfaction that he wrote to the duke to say that it was his intention to become a friar ; and yet he had no sooner got into the place, than he addressed a letter to the Inquisition at Rome, beseeching it to desire permission for him to come to that city, in order to clear himself from the charges of his enemies. He also wrote to two other friends, requesting them to further his petition ; and adding that the duke was enraged with him in consequence of the anger of the Grand Duke of Tuscany, who, it is supposed, had accused Tasso of having revealed to Alfonso some indecent epithet which his highness had applied to him.* These letters were undoubtedly inter-

---

* The application is the conjecture of Black, vol. i., p. 317. Serassi suppressed the whole passage. The indecent word would have been known but for the delicacy or courtliness of Muratori, who substituted an *et-cetera* in its place, observing, that he had "covered" with it "an

cepted, for they were found among the secret
archives of Modena, the only principality ultimately remaining in the Este family; so that,
agreeably to the saying of listeners hearing no
good of themselves, if Alfonso did not know the
epithet before, he learnt it then. The reader
may conceive his feelings. Tasso, too, at the
same time, was plaguing him with letters to
similar purpose; and it is observable, that
while in those which he sent to Rome he
speaks of Cosmo de' Medici as "Grand Duke,"
he takes care in the others to call him simply
the "Duke of Florence." Alfonso had been
exasperated to the last degree at Cosmo's having had the epithet "Grand" added by the
Pope to his ducal title; and the reader may
imagine the little allowance that would be made
by a haughty and angry prince for the rebellious
courtesy thus shown to a detested rival. Tasso,
furthermore, who had not only an infantine
hatred of bitter "physic," but reasonably
thought the fashion of the age for giving it a
ridiculous one, begged hard, in a manner which
it is humiliating to witness, that he might not
be drenched with medicine. The duke at length

indecent word not fit to be printed" (" sotto quell' *el-
cetera* ho io coperta un' indecente parola, che non era
lecito di lasciar correre alle stampe."—"Opera del Tasso,"
vol. xvi., p. 114). By "covered" he seems to have meant
blotted out, for in the latest edition of Tasso the *el-cetera*
is retained.

forbade his writing to him any more; and
Tasso, whose fears of every kind of ill usage
had been wound up to a pitch unbearable,
watched an opportunity when he was carelessly
guarded, and fled at once from the convent and
Ferrara.

The unhappy poet selected the loneliest ways
he could find, and directed his course to the
kingdom of Naples, where his sister lived. He
was afraid of pursuit; he probably had little
money; and considering his ill health and his
dread of the Inquisition, it is pitiable to think
what he may have endured while picking his
long way through the back states of the Church
and over the mountains of Abruzzo, as far as
the Gulf of Naples. For better security, he exchanged clothes with a shepherd; and as he
feared even his sister at first, from doubting
whether she still loved him, his interview with
her was in all its circumstances painfully dramatic. Cornelia Tasso, now a widow, with two
sons, was still residing at Sorrento, where the
poet, casting his eyes around him as he proceeded towards the house, must have beheld with
singular feelings of wretchedness the lovely
spots in which he had been a happy little boy.
He did not announce himself at once. He
brought letters, he said, from the lady's brother;
and it is affecting to think, that whether his

sister might or might not have retained otherwise any personal recollection of him since
that time (for he had not seen her in the interval), his disguise was completed by the altera-
tions which sorrow had made in his appearance.
For, at all events, she did not know him. She
saw in him nothing but a haggard stranger who
was acquainted with the writer of the letters,
and to whom they referred for particulars of the
risk which her brother ran, unless she could
afford him her protection. These particulars
were given by the stranger with all the pathos
of the real man, and the loving sister fainted
away. On her recovery, the visitor said what
he could to reassure her, and then by degrees
discovered himself. Cornelia welcomed him in
the tenderest manner. She did all that he desired; and gave out to her friends that the gentleman was a cousin from Bergamo, who had
come to Naples on family affairs.

For a little while the affection of his sister,
and the beauty and freshness of Sorrento, rendered the mind of Tasso more easy: but his
restlessness returned. He feared he had mor-
tally offended the Duke of Ferrara; and, with
his wonted fluctuation of purpose, he now
wished to be restored to his presence for the
very reason he had run away from it. He did
not know with what vengeance he might be

pursued. He wrote to the duke, but received no answer. The Duchess of Urbino was equally silent. Leonora alone responded, but with no encouragement. These appearances only made him the more anxious to dare or to propitiate his doom; and he accordingly determined to put himself in the duke's hands. His sister entreated him in vain to alter his resolution. He quitted her before the autumn was over, and, proceeding to Rome, went directly to the house of the duke's agent there, who, in concert with the Ferrarese ambassador, gave his master advice of the circumstance. Gonzaga, however, and another good friend, Cardinal Albano, doubted whether it would be wise in the poet to return to Ferrara under any circumstances. They counselled him to be satisfied with being pardoned at a distance, and with having his papers and other things returned to him, and the two friends immediately wrote to the duke requesting as much. The duke apparently acquiesced in all that was desired; but he said that the illness of his sister, the Duchess of Urbino, delayed the procuration of the papers, which, it seems, were chiefly in her hands. The upshot was that the papers did not come; and Tasso, with a mixture of rage and fear, and perhaps for more reasons than he has told, became uncontrollably desirous of retracing the rest of his steps to Ferrara. Love may have been among these reasons—probably was ; though it does not follow that the passion must have been for a princess. The poet now, therefore, petitioned to that effect, and Alfonso wrote again and said he might come, but only on condition of his again undergoing the ducal course of medicine, adding that if he did not he was to be finally expelled from his highness' territories.

He was graciously received—too graciously, it would seem for his equanimity ; for it gave him such a flow of spirits that the duke appears to have thought it necessary to repress them. The unhappy poet, at this, began to have some of his old suspicions, and the unaccountable detention of his papers confirmed them. He made an effort to keep the suspicions down, but it was by means, unfortunately, of drowning them in wine and jollity, and this gave him such a fit of sickness as had nearly been his death. He recovered, only to make a fresh stir about his papers, and a still greater one about his poems in general, which, though his "Jerusalem" was yet only known in manuscript, and not even his "Aminta" published, he believed ought to occupy the attention of mankind. People at Ferrara, therefore, not foreseeing the respect that posterity would entertain for the poet, and having no great desire perhaps to encourage a man who claimed to be a rival of their countryman Ariosto, now began to consider their Neapolitan guest not merely an ingenious and pitiable, but an overweening and tiresome enthusiast. The court, however, still seemed to be interested in its panegyrist, though Tasso feared that Alfonso meant to burn his "Jerusalem." Alfonso, on the other hand, is supposed to have feared that he would burn it himself, and the ducal praises with it. The papers, at all events, apparently including the only fair copy of the poem, were constantly withheld, and Tasso, in a new fit of despair, again quitted Ferrara. This mystery of the papers is certainly very extraordinary.

The poet's first steps were to Mantua, where he met with no such reception as encouraged him to stay. He then went to Urbino, but did not stop long. The prince it is true, was very gracious, and bandages for a cautery were applied by the fair hands of his highness' sister, but, though the nurse enchanted, the surgery frightened him. The hapless poet found himself pursued wherever he went by the tormenting beneficence of medicine. He escaped, and went to Turin. He had no passport, and presented, besides, so miserable an appearance, that the people at the gates roughly refused him admittance. He was well received, however, at court; and as he had begun to acknowledge that he was subject to humors and delusions, and wrote to say as much to Cardinal Albano, who returned him a most excellent and affecting letter, full of the kindest regard and good counsel, his friends entertained a hope that he would become tranquil. But he disappointed them. He again applied to Alfonso for permission to return to Ferrara—again received it, though on worse than the old conditions—and again found himself in that city in, the beginning of the year 1579, delighted at seeing a brilliant assemblage from all quarters of Italy on occasion of a new marriage of the duke's (with a princess of Mantua). He made up his mind to think that nothing could be denied him, at such a moment by the bridegroom whom he meant to honor and glorify.

Alas! the very circumstance to which he looked for success, tended to throw him into the greatest of his calamities. Alfonso was to be married the day after the poet's arrival. He was therefore too busy to attend to him. The princesses did not attend to him. Nobody attended to him. He again applied in vain for his papers. He regretted his return; became anxious to be any where else; thought himself not only neglected but derided; and at length became excited to a pitch of frenzy. He broke forth into the most unmeasured invectives against the duke, even in public; invoked curses on his head and that of his whole race; retracted all he had ever said in the praise of any of them, prince or otherwise; and pronounced him and his whole court "a parcel of ingrates, rascals, and poltroons." * The outbreak was reported to the duke; and the consequence was, that the poet was sent to the hospital of St. Anne, an establishment for the reception of the poor and lunatic, where he remained (with the exception of a few unaccountable leave-days) upwards of seven years. This melancholy event happened in the March of the year 1579.

Tasso was stunned by this blow as much as if he had never done or suffered any thing to expect it. He could at first do nothing but wonder and bewail himself, and implore to be set free. The duke answered, that he must be cured first. Tasso replied by fresh entreaties; the duke returned the same answers. The unhappy poet had recourse to every friend, prince, and great man he could think of, to join his entreaties; he sought refuge in composition, but still entreated; he occasionally reproached and

---

* Black's version (vol. ii., p. 58) is not strong enough. The words in Serassi are "una ciurma di poltroni, ingrati, e ribaldi," ii., p. 33.

even bantered the duke in some of his letters to
his friends, all of which, doubtless, were opened ;
but still he entreated, flattered, adored, all to no
purpose, for seven long years and upwards.   In
time he became subject to maniacal illusions ;
so that if he was not actually mad before, he
was now considered so.   He was not only visited with sights and sounds, such as many people
have experienced whose brains have been over-
excited, but he fancied himself haunted by a
sprite, and become the sport of "magicians."
The sprite stole his things, and the magicians
would not let him get well.   He had a vision
such as Benvenuto Cellini had, of the Virgin
Mary in her glory ; and his nights were so miserable, that he ate too much in order that he
might sleep.   When he was temperate, he lay
awake.   Sometimes he felt "as if a horse had
thrown himself on him."   "Have pity on me,"
he says to the friend to whom he gives these
affecting accounts ; "I am miserable, because
the world is unjust." *

The physicians advised him to leave off wine ;
but he says he could not do that, though he was
content to use it in moderation.   In truth he
required something to support him against the
physicians themselves, for they continued to
exhaust his strength by their medicines, and

* "Opere," vol. xiv., pp. 158, 174, etc.

could not supply the want of it with air and freedom. He had ringings in the ears, vomits, and fluxes of blood. It would be ludicrous, if it were not deplorably pathetic, to hear so great a man, in the commonest medical terms, now protesting against the eternal drenches of these practitioners, now humbly submitting to them, and now entreating like a child, that they might at least not be " so bitter." The physicians, with the duke at their head, were as mad for their rhubarbs and lancets as the quacks in Molière; and nothing but the very imagination that had nearly sacrificed the poet's life to their ignorance could have hindered him from dashing his head against the wall, and leaving them to the execrations of posterity. It is the only occasion in which the noble profession of medicine has not appeared in wise and beneficent connection with the sufferings of men of letters. Why did Ferrara possess no Brocklesby in those days? no Garth, Mead, Warren, or Southwood Smith?

Tasso enabled himself to endure his imprisonment with composition. He supported it with his poetry and his poem, and what, alas ! he had been too proud of during his liberty, the praises of his admirers. His genius brought him gifts from princes, and some money from the booksellers: it supported him even against his critics. During his confinement the "Jerusalem Delivered" was first published; though, to his grief, from a surreptitious and mutilated copy. But it was followed by a storm of applause; and if this was succeeded by as great a storm of objection and controversy, still the healthier part of his faculties were roused, and he exasperated his critics and astonished the world by showing how coolly and learnedly the poor, wild, imprisoned genius could discuss the most intricate questions of poetry and philosophy. The disputes excited by his poem are generally supposed to have done him harm; but the conclusion appears to be ill founded. They diverted his thoughts, and made him conscious of his powers and his fame. I doubt whether he would have been better for entire approbation: it would have put him in a state of elevation, unfit for what he had to endure. He had found his pen his great solace, and he had never employed it so well. It would be incredible what a heap of things he wrote in this complicated torment of imprisonment, sickness, and "physic," if habit and mental activity had not been sufficient to account for much greater wonders. His letters to his friends and others would make a good-sized volume; those to his critics, another; sonnets and odes, a third; and his Dialogues after the manner of Plato, two more. Perhaps a good half of all he wrote was written in this hospital of St. Anne; and he studied as well as composed, and had to read all that was written at the time, *pro* and *con*, in the discussions about his "Jerusalem," which, in the latest edition of his works, amount to three out of six volumes octavo! Many of the occasions, however, of his poems, as well as letters, are most painful to think of, their object having been to exchange praise for money. And it is distressing, in the letters, to see his other little wants, and the fluctuations and moods of his mind. Now he is angry about some book not restored, or some gift promised and delayed. Now he is in want of some books to be lent him; now of some praise to comfort him; now of a little fresh linen. He is very thankful for visits, for respectful letters, for "sweetmeats"; and greatly puzzled to know what to do with the bad sonnets and panegyrics that are sent him. They were sometimes too much even for the allowed ultra courtesies of Italian acknowledgement. His compliments to most people are varied with astonishing grace and ingenuity; his accounts of his condition often sufficient to bring the tears into the manliest eyes; and his ceaseless and vain efforts to procure his liberation mortifying when we think of himself,

and exasperating when we think of the petty
despot who detained him in so long, so degrad-
ing, and so worse than useless confinement.

Tasso could not always conceal his contempt
of his imprisoner from the ducal servants. Alfonso excelled the grandiloquent poet himself
in his love of pomp and worship; and as he
had no particular merits to warrant it, his vic-
tim bantered his love of titles. He says, in a
letter to the duke's steward : "If it is the pleasure of the Most Serene Signor Duke, Most
Clement and Most Invincible, to keep me in
prison, may I beg that he will have the goodness to return certain little things of mine,
which his Most Invincible, Most Clement, and
Most Serene Highness has so often promised
me."*

But these were rare ebullitions of gayety, perhaps rather of bitter despair. A playful address
to a cat to lend him her eyes to write by, during
some hour in which he happened to be without
a light (for it does not appear to have been denied him), may be taken as more probable
evidence of a mind relieved at the moment,
though the necessity for the relief may have

* " Prego V. Signoria che si contenti, se piace al Serenis-
simo Signor Duca, Clementissimo ed Invitissimo, che io
stia in prigione, di farmi dar le poche robicciole mie, che
S. A. Invitissima, Clementissima, Serenissima m' ha
promesse tante volte," etc.—" Opere," vol. xiv., p. 6.

been very sad. But the style in which he generally alludes to his situation is far different. He continually begs his correspondents to pity him, to pray for him, to attribute his errors to infirmity. He complains of impaired memory, and acknowledges that he has become subject to the deliriums formerly attributed to him by the enemies that helped to produce them. Petitioning the native city of his ancestors (Bergamo) to intercede for him with the duke, he speaks of the writer as "this unhappy person," and subscribes himself,—

"Most illustrious Signors, your affectionate servant, Torquato Tasso, a prisoner, and infirm, in the hospital of St. Anne in Ferrara."

In one of his addresses to Alfonso, he says most affectingly :

"I have sometimes attributed much to myself, and considered myself as somebody. But now, seeing in how many ways imagination has imposed on me, I suspect that it has also deceived me in this opinion of my own consequence. Indeed, methinks the past has been a dream ; and hence I am resolved to rely on my imagination no longer."

Alfonso made no answer.

The causes of Tasso's imprisonment, and its long duration, are among the puzzles of biography. The prevailing opinion, notwithstanding the opposition made to it by Serassi and Black, is, that the poet made love to the Princess Leonora—perhaps was beloved by her ; and that her brother the duke punished him for his arrogance. This was the belief of his earliest biographer, Manso, who was intimately acquainted with the poet in his latter days; and from Manso (though he did not profess to receive the information from Tasso, but only to gather it from his poems) it spread all over Europe. Milton took it on trust from him ; * and so have our English translators Hoole and Wiffen. The Abbé de Charnes, however, declined to do so ; † and Montaigne, who saw the poet in St. Anne's hospital, says nothing of the love at all. He attributes his condition to poetical excitement, hard study, and the meeting of the extremes of wisdom and folly. The philosopher, however, speaks of the poet's having survived his reason, and become unconscious both of himself and his works, which the reader knows to be untrue. He does not appear to have conversed with Tasso. The poet was only shown him ; probably at a sick moment, or by a new and ignorant official.‡ Muratori,

* " Altera Torquatum cepit Leonora poetam," etc.
† " Vie du Tasse," 1695, p. 51.
‡ In the " Apology for Raimond de Sebonde ;" Essays, vol. ii., ch. 12.

who was in the service of the Este family at
Modena, tells us, on the authority of an old acquaintance who knew contemporaries of Tasso,
that the "good Torquato" finding himself one
day in company with the duke and his sister,
and going close to the princess in order to answer some question which she had put to him,
was so transported by an impulse "more than
poetical," as to give her a kiss ; upon which the
duke, who had observed it, turned about to his
gentleman, and said, "What a pity to see so
great a man distracted!" and so ordered him
to be locked up.* But this writer adds, that he
does not know what to think of the anecdote :
he neither denies nor admits it. Tiraboschi,
who was also in the service of the Este family,
doubts the truth of the anecdote, and believes
that the duke shut the poet up solely for fear
lest his violence should do harm.† Serassi, the
second biographer of Tasso, who dedicated his
book to an Este princess inimical to the poet's
memory, attributes the confinement, on his own
showing, to the violent words he had uttered
against his master.‡ Walker, the author of the

* In his Letter to Zeno,—"Opere del Tasso," xvi.,
p. 118.

† "Storia della Poesia Italiana" (Matthias' edition),
vol. iii., part i., p. 236.

‡ Serassi is very peremptory, and even abusive. He
charges every body who has said any thing to the contrary with imposture. "Egli non v' ha dubbio, che le

"Memoir on Italian Tragedy," says, that the
life by Serassi himself induced him to credit
the love-story : * so does Ginguéné.† Black,
forgetting the age and illnesses of hundreds of
enamoured ladies, and the distraction of lovers
at all times, derides the notion of passion on
either side : because, he argues, Tasso was subject to frenzies, and Leonora forty-two years of
age, and not in good-health.‡ What would
Madame d'Houdetot have said to him ? or Made-
moiselle L'Espinasse? or Mrs. Inchbald, who
used to walk up and down Sackville Street in
order that she might see Dr. Warren's light in
his window? Foscolo was a believer in the
love ;§ Sismondi admits it; ‖ and Rosini, the
editor of the latest edition of the poet's works,
is passionate for it. He wonders how any body

troppe imprudenti e temerarie parole, che il Tasso si
lasciò uscir di bocca in questo incontro, furone la sola
cagione della sua prigionia, e ch' è mera favola ed *im-
postura* tutto ciò, che diversamente è stato affermato e
scritto da altri in tale proposito." Vol. ii., p. 33. But we
have seen that the good Abbé could practise a little im-
position himself.

* Black, ii., 88.   † "Hist. Litt. d'Italie," v., 243, etc.

‡ Vol. ii., p. 89.

§ Such at least is my impression ; but I cannot call the
evidence to mind.

‖ "Literature of the South of Europe " (Roscoe's translation), vol. ii., p. 165. To show the loose way in which
the conclusions of a man's own mind are presented as
facts admitted by others, Sismondi says, that Tasso's
" passion " was the cause of his return to Ferrara. There
is not a tittle of evidence to show for it.

can fail to discern it in a number of passages, which, in truth, may mean a variety of other loves ; and he insists much upon certain loose verses (*lascivi*) which the poet, among his various accounts of the origin of his imprisonment, assigns as the cause, or one of the causes, of it. *

I confess, after a reasonable amount of inquiry into this subject, that I can find no proofs whatsoever of Tasso's having made love to Leonora ; though I think it highly probable. I believe the main cause of the duke's proceedings was the poet's own violence of behavior and incontinence of speech. I think it very likely that, in the course of the poetical lovemaking to various ladies, which was almost identical in that age with addressing them in verse, Torquato, whether he was in love or not, took more liberties with the princesses than Alfonso approved ; and it is equally probable, that one of those liberties consisted in his indulging his imagination too far. It is not even impossible, that more gallantry may have been going on at court than Alfonso could endure to

* " Saggio sugli Amori," etc., *ut. sup.*, p. 84, and *passim*. As specimens of the learned professor's reasoning, it may be observed that whenever the words *humble, daring, high, noble*, and *royal*, occur in the poet's love-verses, he thinks they *must* allude to the Princess Leonora ; and he argues, that Alfonso never could have been so angry with any "versi lascivi," if they had not had the same direction.

see alluded to, especially by an ambitious pen.
But there is no evidence that such was the case.
Tasso, as a gentleman, could not have hinted
at such a thing on the part of a princess of staid
reputation; and, on the other hand, the "love"
he speaks of as entertained by her for him, and
warranting the application to her for money in
case of his death, was too plainly worded to
mean any thing but love in the sense of friendly regard. "Per amor mio" is an idiomatical
expression, meaning "for my sake;" a strong
one, no doubt, and such as a proud man like
Alfonso might think a liberty, but not at all of
necessity an amatory boast. If it was, its very
effrontery and vanity were presumptions of its
falsehood. The lady whom Tasso alludes to in
the passage quoted on his first confinement is
complained of for her coldness towards him;
and, unless this was itself a gentlemanly blind,
it might apply to fifty other ladies besides the
princess. The man who assaulted him in the
streets, and who is supposed to have been the
violator of his papers, need not have found any
secrets of love in them. The servant at whom
he aimed the knife or the dagger might be as
little connected with such matters; and the
sonnets which the poet said he wrote for a
friend, and which he desired to be buried with
him, might be alike innocent of all reference to

Leonora, whether he wrote them for a friend or not. Leonora's death took place during the poet's confinement; and, lamented as she was by the verse-writers according to custom, Tasso wrote nothing on the event. This silence has been attributed to the depth of his passion; but how is the fact proved? and why may it not have been occasioned by there having been no passion at all?

All that appears certain is, that Tasso spoke violent and contemptuous words against the duke; that he often spoke ill of him in his letters; that he endeavored, not with perfect ingenuousness, to exchange his service for that of another prince; that he asserted his madness to have been pretended in the first instance purely to gratify the duke's whim for thinking it so (which was one of the reasons perhaps why Alfonso, as he complained, would not believe a word he said); and finally, that, whether the madness was or was not so pretended, it unfortunately became a confirmed though milder form of mania, during a long confinement.

Alfonso, too proud to forgive the poet's contempt, continued thus to detain him, partly perhaps because he was not sorry to have a pretext for revenge, partly because he did not know what to do with him consistently either with his own or the poet's safety. He had not been generous enough to put Tasso above his wants ; he had not address enough to secure his respect ; he had not merit enough to overlook his reproaches. If Tasso had been as great a man as he was a poet, Alfonso would not have been reduced to these perplexities. The poet would have known how to settle quietly down on his small court-income, and wait patiently in the midst of his beautiful visions for what fortune had or had not in store for him. But in truth¦ he, as well as the duke, was weak ; they made a bad business of it between them ; and Alfonso the Second closed the accounts of the Este family with the Muses, by keeping his panegyrist seven years in a mad-house, to the astonishment of posterity, and the destruction of his own claims to renown.

It does not appear that Tasso was confined in any such dungeon as they now exhibit in Ferrara. The conduct of the Prior of the Hospital is more doubtful. His name was Agostino Mosti ; and, strangely enough, he was the person who had raised a monument to Ariosto, of whom he was an enthusiastic admirer. To this predilection has been attributed his alleged cruelty to the stranger from Sorrento, who dared to emulate the fame of his idol,—an extraordinary, though perhaps not incredible, mode of showing a critic's regard for poetry. But Tasso, while he laments his severity, wonders at it in a man so well-bred and so imbued with literature, and thinks it can only have originated in "orders."* Perhaps there were faults of temper on both sides ; and Mosti, not liking his office, forgot the allowance to be made for that of a prisoner and sick man. His nephew, Giulio Mosti, became strongly attached to the poet, and was a great comfort to him.

At length the time for liberation arrived. In the summer of 1586, Don Vincenzo Gonzaga, Prince of Mantua, kinsman of the poet's friend Scipio, came to Ferrara for the purpose of complimenting Alfonso's heir on his nuptials. The whole court of Mantua, with hereditary regard for Tasso, whose father had been one of their ornaments, were desirous of having him among them ; and the prince extorted Alfonso's permission to take him away, on condition (so hard did he find this late concession to humanity, and so fearful was he of losing the dignity of jailor) that his deliverer should not allow him to quit Mantua without obtaining leave. A young and dear friend, his most frequent visitor, Antonio Constantini, secretary to the Tuscan ambassador, went to St. Anne's to prepare

* "Opere," vol. xvii., p. 32.

the captive by degrees for the good news. He told him that he really might look for his release in the course of a few days. The sensitive poet, now a premature old man of forty-two, was thrown into a transport of mingled delight and anxiety. He had been disappointed so often that he could scarcely believe his good fortune. In a day or two he writes thus to his visitor :

"Your kindness, my dear friend, has so accustomed me to your precious and frequent visits, that I have been all day long at the window expecting your coming to comfort me as you are wont. But since you have not yet arrived, and in order not to remain altogether without consolation, I visit you with this letter. It encloses a sonnet to the ambassador, written with a trembling hand, and in such a manner that he will not, perhaps, have less difficulty in reading it than I had in writing."

Two days afterwards, the prince himself came again, requested of the poet some verses on a given subject, expressed his esteem for his genius and virtues, and told him that, on his return to Mantua, he should have the pleasure of conducting him to that city. Tasso lay awake almost all night, composing the verses ; and next day enclosed them, with a letter, in another to Constantini, ardently begging him to keep the prince in mind of his promise. The prince had not forgotten it; and two or three days afterwards, the order for the release arrived, and Tasso quitted his prison. He had been confined seven years, two months and several days. He awaited the prince's departure for a week or two in his friend's abode, paying no visits, probably from inability to endure so much novelty. Neither was he inclined or sent for to pay his respects to the duke. Two such parties could hardly have been desirous to look on each other. The duke must especially have disliked the thought of it; though Tasso afterwards fancied otherwise, and that he was offended at his non-appearance. But his letters, unfortunately, differ with themselves on this point, as on most others. About the middle of July, 1586, the poet quitted Ferrara forever.

At Mantua, Tasso was greeted with all the honors and attentions which his love of distinction could desire. The good old duke, the friend of his father, ordered handsome apartments to be provided for him in the palace; the prince made him presents of costly attire, including perfumed silken hose (kindred elegancies to the Italian gloves of Queen Elizabeth); the princess and her mother-in-law were declared admirers of his poetry; the courtiers

caressed the favorite of their masters ; Tasso
found literary society ; he pronounced the very
bread and fruit, the fish and the flesh, excellent ; the wines were sharp and brisk ("such as
his father was fond of") ; and even the physician was admirable, for he ordered confections.
One might imagine, if circumstances had not
proved the cordial nature of the Gonzaga family, and the real respect and admiration entertained for the poet's genius by the greatest men
of the time, in spite of the rebuke it had received from Alfonso, that there had been a con-
federacy to mock and mystify him, after the
fashion of the duke and duchess with Don
Quixote (the only blot, by the way, in the book
of Cervantes ; if, indeed, he did not intend it as
a satire on the mystifiers).

For a while, in short, the liberated prisoner
thought himself happy. He corrected his prose
works, resumed and finished the tragedy of
Torrismond, which he had begun some years
before, corresponded with princes, and completed and published a narrative poem left un-
finished by his father. Torquato was as loving
a son as Mozart or Montaigne. Whenever he
had a glimpse of felicity, he appears to have
associated the idea of it with that of his father.
In the conclusion of his fragment, "O del
grand' Apennino," he affectingly begs pardon

of his blessed spirit for troubling him with his earthly griefs.*

But, alas, what had been an indulgence of self-esteem had now become the habit of a disease ; and in the course of a few months the restless poet began to make his old discovery, that he was not sufficiently cared for. The prince had no leisure to attend to him ; the nobility did not " yield him the first place," or at least (he adds) they did not allow him to be treated "externally as their equal" ; and he candidly confessed that he could not live in a place where such was the custom.† He felt also, naturally enough, however well it might have been intended, that it was not pleasant to be confined to the range of the city of Mantua, attended by a servant, even though he con-

---

* " Padre, o buon padre, che dal ciel rimiri,
Egro e morto ti piansi, e ben tu il sai ;
E gemendo scaldai
La tomba e il letto. Or che negli altri giri
Tu godi, a te si deve onor, non lutto :
A me versato il mio dolor sia tutto."

O father, my good father, looking now
On thy poor son from heaven, well knowest thou
What scalding tears I shed
Upon thy grave, upon thy dying bed ;
But since thou dwellest in the happy skies,
'T is fit I raise to thee no sorrowing eyes :
Be all my grief on my own head.

† " Non posso viver in città, ove tutti i nobili, o non mi concedano i primi luoghi, o almeno non si contentino che la cosa in quel che appartiene a queste esteriori dimostrazioni, vada del pari."—" Opere," vol. xiii., p. 153.

fessed that he was now subject to "frenzy." He contrived to stay another half year by help of a brilliant carnival and of the select society of the prince's court, who were evidently most kind to him ; but at the end of the twelvemonth he was in Bergamo among his relations. The prince gave him leave to go ; and the Cavaliere Tasso, his kinsman, sent his chariot on purpose to fetch him.

Here again he found himself at a beautiful country-seat, which the family of Tasso still possesses near that city ; and here again, in the house of his father, he proposed to be happy, "having never desired," he says, "any journey more earnestly than this." He left it in the course of a month, to return to Mantua.

And it was only to wander still. Mantua he quitted in less than two months to go to Rome, in spite of the advice of his best friends. He vindicated the proceeding by a hope of obtaining some permanent settlement from the Pope. He took Loretto by the way, to refresh himself with devotion ; arrived in a transport at Rome ; got nothing from the Pope (the hard-minded Sixtus the Fifth) ; and in the spring of the next year, in the triple hope of again embracing his sister, and recovering the dowry of his mother and the confiscated property of his father, he proceeded to Naples.

Naples was in its most beautiful vernal condition, and the Neapolitans welcomed the poet with all honor and glory; but his sister, alas, was dead; he got none of his father's property, nor (till too late) any of his mother's; and before the year was out, he was again in Rome. He acquired in Naples, however, another friend, as attached to him and as constant in his attentions as his beloved Constantini, to wit, Giambattista Manso, Marquis of Villa, who became his biographer, and who was visited and praised for his good offices by Milton. In the society of this gentleman he seemed for a short while to have become a new man. He entered into field sports, listened to songs and music, nay, danced, says Manso, with "the girls." (One fancies a poetical Dr. Johnson with the two country damsels on his knees.) In short, good air and freedom, and no medicine, had conspired with the lessons of disappointment to give him, before he died, a glimpse of the power to be pleased. He had not got rid of all his spiritual illusions, even those of a melancholy nature; but he took the latter more quietly, and had grown so comfortable with the race in general, that he encouraged them. He was so entirely freed from his fears of the Inquisition and of charges of magic, that whereas he had formerly been anxious to show that he meant nothing but a poetical fancy by the spirit which he introduced as communing with him in his dialogue entitled the "Messenger," he now maintained its reality against the arguments of his friend Manso; and these arguments gave rise to the most poetical scene in his history. He told Manso that he should have ocular testimony of the spirit's existence; and accordingly one day while they were sitting together at the marquis' fireside, "he turned his eyes," says Manso, "towards a window, and held them a long time so intensely on it, that, when I called him, he did not answer. At last, 'Behold,' said he, 'the friendly spirit which has courteously come to talk with me. Lift up your eyes and see the truth.' I turned my eyes thither immediately (continues the marquis); but though I endeavored to look as keenly as I could, I beheld nothing but the rays of the sun, which streamed through the panes of the window into the chamber. Whilst I still looked around, without beholding any object, Torquato began to hold, with this unknown something, a most lofty converse. I heard, indeed, and saw nothing but himself; nevertheless his words, at one time questioning, at another replying, were such as take place between those who reason strictly on some important subject. And from what was said by the one, the reply

of the other might be easily comprehended by
the intellect, although it was not heard by the
ear. The discourses were so lofty and marvellous, both by the sublimity of their topics
and a certain unwonted manner of talking, that,
exalted above myself in a kind of ecstasy, I did
not dare to interrupt them, nor ask Tasso about
the spirit, which he had announced to me, but
which I did not see. In this way, while I listened between stupefaction and rapture, a considerable time had elapsed; till at last the spirit
departed, as I learned from the words of Torquato; who, turning to me, said, 'From this
day forward all your doubts will have vanished
from your mind.' 'Nay,' said I, 'they are
rather increased; since, though I have heard
many things worthy of marvel, I have seen
nothing of what you promised to show me to
dispel them.' He smiled, and said, 'You have
seen and heard more of him than perhaps——,'
and here he paused. Fearful of importuning
him with new questions, the discourse ended;
and the only conclusion I can draw is, what I
before said, that it is more likely his visions or
frenzies will disorder my own mind than that
I shall extirpate his true or imaginary opinion.'' *

Did the "smile" of Tasso at the close of this

* Black, vol. ii., p. 240.

extraordinary scene, and the words which he omitted to add, signify that his friend had seen and heard more, perhaps, than the poet *would have liked* to explain? Did he mean that he himself alone had been seen and heard, and was author of the whole dialogue? Perhaps he did; for credulity itself can impose—can take pleasure in seeing others as credulous itself. On the other hand, enough has become known in our days of the phenomena of morbid perception, to render Tasso's actual belief in such visions not at all surprising. It is not uncommon for the sanest people of delicate organization to see faces before them while going to sleep, sometimes in fantastical succession. A stronger exercise of this disposition in temperaments more delicate will enlarge the face to figure; and there can be no question that an imagination so heated as Tasso's, so full of the speculations of the later Platonists, and accompanied by a state of body so " nervous," and a will so bent on its fancies, might embody whatever he chose to behold. The dialogue he could as easily read in the vision's looks, whether he heard it or not with ears. If Nicholay, the Prussian bookseller, who saw crowds of spiritual people go through his rooms, had been a poet, and possessed of as wilful an imagination as Tasso, he might have gifted them all with *speaking*

countenances as easily as with coats and waist-
coats. Swedenborg founded a religion on this
morbid faculty ; and the Catholics worship a
hundred stories of the like sort in the lives of the
Saints, many of which are equally true and false;
false in reality, though true in supposition.
Luther himself wrote and studied till he saw the
Devil ; only the great reformer retained enough
of his naturally sturdy health and judgment to
throw an inkstand at Satan's head,—a thing
that philosophy has been doing ever since.

Tasso's principal residence while at Naples
had been in the beautiful monastery of Mount
Olivet, on which the good monks begged he
would write them a poem ; which he did. A
cold reception at Rome, and perhaps the difference of the air, brought back his old lamenta-
tions ; but here again a monastery gave him
refuge, and he set himself down to correct his
former works and compose new ones. He
missed, however, the comforts of society and
amusement which he had experienced at Naples.
Nevertheless, he did not return thither. He
persuaded himself that it was necessary to be in
Rome in order to expedite the receipt of some
books and manuscripts from Bergamo and other
places ; but his restlessness desired novelty. He
thus slipped back from the neighborhood of
Rome to the city itself, and from the city back

to the monastery, his friends in both places being probably tired of his instability. He thought
of returning to Mantua ; but a present from the
Grand Duke of Tuscany, accompanied by an
invitation to his court, drew him, in one of his
short-lived transports, to Florence. He returned,
in spite of the best and most generous reception, to Rome ; then left Rome for Mantua, on
invitation from his ever-kind deliverer from
prison, now the reigning duke ; tired again, even
of him ; returned to Rome ; then once more to
Naples, where the Prince of Conca, Grand Admiral of the kingdom, lodged and treated him
like an equal ; but he grew suspicious of the
admiral, and went to live with his friend Manso;
quitted Manso for Rome again ; was treated
with reverence on the way, like Ariosto, by a
famous leader of banditti ; was received at Rome
into the Vatican itself, in the apartments of
his friend Cintio Aldobrandino, nephew of the
new Pope Clement the Eighth, where his hopes
now seemed to be raised at once to their highest
and most reasonable pitch ; but fell ill, and was
obliged to go back to Naples for the benefit of
the air. A life so strangely erratic to the last
(for mortal illness was approaching) is perhaps
unique in the history of men of letters, and
might be therefore worth recording even in that
of a less man than Tasso ; but when we recol-

lect that this poet, in spite of all his weaknesses, and notwithstanding the enemies they provoked and the friends they cooled, was really almost adored for his genius in his own time, and instead of refusing jewels one day and soliciting a ducat the next, might have settled down almost anywhere in quiet and glory, if he had but possessed the patience to do so,—it becomes an association of weakness with power, and of adversity with the means of prosperity, the absurdity of which admiration itself can only drown in pity.

He now took up his abode in another monastery, that of San Severino, where he was comforted by the visits of his friend Manso, to whom he had lately inscribed a dialogue on "Friendship"; for he continued writing to the last. He had also the consolation, such as it was, of having the lawsuit for his mother's dowry settled in his favor, though under circumstances that rendered it of little importance, and only three months before his death. So strangely did Fortune seem to take delight in sporting with a man of genius, who had thought both too much of her and too little; too much for pomp's sake, and too little in prudence. Among his new acquaintances were the young Marino, afterwards the corrupter of Italian poetry, and the Prince of Venosa, an ama-

teur composer of music. The dying poet wrote
madrigals for him so much to his satisfaction,
that, being about to marry into the house of
Este, he wished to reconcile him with the Duke
of Ferrara ; and Tasso, who to the last moment
of his life seems never to have been able to resist the chance of resuming old quarters, apparently from the double temptation of renouncing
them, wrote his old master a letter full of respects and regrets. But the duke, who himself
died in the course of the year, was not to be
moved from his silence. The poet had given
him the last possible offence by recasting his
"Jerusalem," omitting the glories of the house
of Este, and dedicating it to another patron.
Alfonso, who had been extravagantly magnificent, though not to poets, had so weakened his
government, that the Pope wrested Ferrara
from the hands of his successor, and reduced
the Este family to the possession of Modena,
which it still holds and dishonors. The duke
and the poet were thus fading away at the same
time; they never met again in this world ; and
a new Dante would have divided them far
enough in the next.*

* The world in general have taken no notice of Tasso's
reconstruction of his " Jerusalem," which he called the
"Gerusalemme Conquistata." It never "obtained," as
the phrase is. It was a mere tribute of his declining
years to bigotry and new acquaintances ; and therefore
I say no more of it.

The last glimpse of honor and glory was now
opening in a very grand manner on the poet—
the last and the greatest, as if on purpose to give
the climax to his disappointments. Cardinal
Cintio requested the Pope to give him the
honor of a coronation. It had been desired
by the poet, it seems, three years before. He
was disappointed of it at that time ; and now
that it was granted, he was disappointed of the
ceremony. Manso says he no longer cared for it ;
and, as he felt himself dying, this is not improbable. Nevertheless he went to Rome for the
purpose ; and though the severity of the winter
there delayed the intention till spring, wealth
and honors seemed determined to come in floods
upon the poor expiring great man, in order to
take away the breath which they had refused to
support. The Pope assigned him a yearly pen-
sion of a hundred scudi ; and the withholders of
his mother's dowry came to an accommodation
by which he was to have an annuity of a hundred ducats, and a considerable sum in hand.
His hand was losing strength enough to close
upon the money. Scarcely was the day for the
coronation about to dawn, when the poet felt
his dissolution approaching. Alfonso's doctors
had killed him at last by superinducing a habit
of medicine-taking, which defeated its purpose.
He requested leave to return to the monastery

of St. Onofrio—wrote a farewell letter to Constantini—received the distinguished honor of a plenary indulgence from the Pope—said (in terms very like what Milton might have used, had he died a Catholic), that "this was the chariot upon which he hoped to go crowned, not with laurel as a poet into the capitol, but with glory as a saint to heaven"—and expired on the 25th of April, 1595, and the fifty-first year of his age, closely embracing the crucifix, and imperfectly uttering the sentence beginning, "Into thy hands, O Lord!"*

Even after death, success mocked him; for the coronation took place on the senseless dead body. The head was wreathed with laurel; a magnificent toga delayed for awhile the shroud; and a procession took place through the city by torchlight, all the inhabitants pouring forth to behold it, and painters crowding over the bier to gaze on the poet's lineaments, from which they produced a multitude of portraits. The corpse was then buried in the church of St. Onofrio; and magnificent monuments talked of, which never appeared. Manso, however, obtained leave to set up a modest tablet; and eight years afterwards a Ferrarese cardinal (Bevilacqua) made what amends he could for

* "In manus tuas Domine." One likes to know the actual words; at least so it appears to me.

his countrymen, by erecting the stately memorial which is still to be seen.

Poor, illustrious Tasso! weak enough to warrant pity from his inferiors—great enough to overshadow in death his once-fancied superiors. He has been a by-word for the misfortunes of genius; but genius was not his misfortune; it was his only good, and might have brought him all happiness. It is the want of genius, as far as it goes, and apart from martyrdoms for conscience' sake, which produces misfortunes even to genius itself—the want of as much wit and balance on the common side of things, as genius is supposed to confine to the uncommon.

Manso has left a minute account of his friend's person and manners. He was tall, even among the tall; had a pale complexion, sunken cheeks, lightish brown hair, head bald at the top, large blue eyes, square forehead, big nose inclining towards the mouth, lips pale and thin, white teeth, delicate white hands, long arms, broad chest and shoulders, legs rather strong than fleshy and the body altogether better proportioned than in good condition; the result, nevertheless, being an aspect of manly beauty and expression, particularly in the countenance, the dignity of which marked him for an extraordinary person even to those who did not know him. His demeanor was grave and deliberate; he laughed seldom ; and though his tongue was prompt, his delivery was slow ; and he was accustomed to repeat his last words. He was an expert in all manly exercises, but not equally graceful ; and the same defect attended his otherwise striking eloquence in public assemblies. His putting to flight the assassins in Ferrara gave him such a reputation for courage, that there went about in his honor a popular couplet :

> " Colla penna e colla spada
> Nessum val quanto Torquato."
>
> For the sword as well as pen
> Tasso is the man of men.

He was a little eater, but not averse to wine, particularly such as combined piquancy with sweetness ; and he always dressed in black.

Manso's account is still more particular, and yet it does not tell all ; for Tasso himself informs us that he stammered, and was near-sighted * ; and a Neapolitan writer who knew him adds to the near-sightedness some visible defect in the eyes.† I should doubt, from what Tasso says

---

* Serassi, ii., 276.

† " Quem, *cernis*, quisquis es, procera statura virum, *luscis* oculis, etc. hic Torquatus est."—Cappacio, " Illustrium Literis Virorum Elogia et Judicia," quoted by Serassi, *ut sup*. The Latin word *luscus*, as well as the Italian *losco*, means, I believe, near-sighted ; but it certainly means also a great deal more ; and unless the word *cernis* (thou beholdst) is a mere form of speech implying a foregone conclusion, it shows that the defect was obvious to the spectator,

in his letters, whether he was fond of speaking in public, notwithstanding his *début* in that line with the "Fifty Amorous Conclusions." Nor does he appear to have been remarkable for his conversation. Manso has left a collection of one hundred of his pithy sayings—a suspicious amount, and unfortunately more than warranting the suspicion ; for almost every one of them is traceable to some other man. They come from the Greek and Latin philosophers, and the apothegms of Erasmus. The two following have the greatest appearance of being genuine :

A Greek, complaining that he had spoken ill of his country, and maintaining that all the virtues in the world had issued out of it, the poet assented ; with the addition, that they had not left one behind them.

A foolish young fellow, garnished with a number of golden chains, coming into a room where he was, and being overheard by him exclaiming, "Is this the great man that was mad?" Tasso said, "Yes ; but that people had never put on him more than one chain at a time."

His character may be gathered, but not perhaps entirely, from what has been written of his life ; for some of his earlier letters show him to have been not quite so grave and refined in his way of talking as readers of the "Jerusalem"

might suppose. He was probably, at that time
of life not so scrupulous in his morals as he professed to be during the greater part of it. His
mother is thought to have died of chagrin and
impatience at being separated so long from her
husband, and not knowing what to do to save
her dowry from her brothers ; and I take her
son to have combined his mother's ultra-sensitive organization with his father's worldly imprudence and unequal spirits. The addition of
the nervous temperament of one parent to the
aspiring nature of the other gave rise to the
poet's trembling eagerness for distinction ; and
Torquato's very love for them both hindered
him from seeing what should have been corrected in the infirmities which he inherited.
Falling from the highest hopes of prosperity
into the most painful afflictions, he thus wanted
solid principles of action to support him, and
was forced to retreat upon an excess of self-
esteem, which allowed his pride to become
a beggar, and his naturally kind, loving, just,
and heroical disposition to condescend to almost
every species of inconsistency. The Duke of
Ferrara, he complains, did not believe a word
he said* ; and the fact is, that, partly from disease, and partly from a want of courage to look

* " Il Signor Duca non crede ad alcuna mia parola,"
—" Opere," xiv., 161.

his defects in the face, he beheld the same things in so many different lights, and according as it suited him at the moment, that, without intending falsehood, his statements are really not to be relied on. He degraded even his verses, sometimes with panegyrics for interest's sake, sometimes out of weak wishes to oblige, of which he was afterwards ashamed; and, with the exception of Constantini, we cannot be sure that any one person praised in them retained his regard in his last days. His suspicion made him a kind of Rousseau; but he was more amiable than the Genevese, and far from being in the habit of talking against old acquaintances, whatever he might have thought of them. It is observable, not only that he never married, but he told Manso he had led a life of entire continence ever since he had entered the walls of his prison, being then in his thirty-fifth year.* Was this out of fidelity to some mistress? or the consequence of a previous life the reverse of continent? or was it from some principle of superstition? He had become a devotee, apparently out of a dread of disbelief; and he remained extremely religious for the rest of his days.

* "Fui da bocca di lui medesimo rassicurato, che dal tempo del suo ritegno in sant' Anna, ch' avenne negli anni trentacinque della sua vita e sedici avanti la morte, egli intieramente fu casto: degli anni primi non mi favellò mai di modo ch' io possa alcuna cosa di certo qui raccontare."—"Opere," xxxiii., 235.

The two unhappiest of Italian poets, Tasso and Dante, were the two most superstitious.

As for the once formidable question concerning the comparative merits of this poet and Ariosto, which anticipated the modern quarrels of the classical and romantic schools, some idea of the treatment which Tasso experienced may be conceived by supposing all that used to be sarcastic and bitter in the periodical party criticism among ourselves some thirty years back collected into one huge vial of wrath, and poured upon the new poet's head. Even the great Galileo, who was a man of wit, bred up in the pure Tuscan school of Berni and Casa, and who was an idolater of Ariosto, wrote, when he was young, a "review" of the "Jerusalem Delivered," which it is painful to read, it is so unjust and contemptuous.* But now that the only final arbiter, posterity, has accepted both the poets, the dispute is surely the easiest thing in the world to settle ; not, indeed, with prejudices of creeds or temperaments, but before any judges thoroughly sympathizing with the two claimants. Its solution is the principle of the greater including the less. For Ariosto errs by having an unbounded circle to move in. His sympathies are unlimited ; and those who

---

* It is to be found in the collected works, *ut supra*, both of the philosopher and the poet.

think him inferior to Tasso only do so in consequence of their own want of sympathy with the vivacities that degrade him in their eyes. Ariosto can be as grave and exalted as Tasso when he pleases, and he could do a hundred things which Tasso never attempted. He is as different in this respect as Shakespeare from Milton. He had far more knowledge of mankind than Tasso, and he was superior in point of taste. But it is painful to make disadvantageous comparisons of one great poet with another. Let us be thankful for Tasso's enchanted gardens, without being forced to vindicate the universal world of his predecessor. Suffice it to bear in mind that the grave poet himself agreed with the rest of the Italians in calling the Ferrarese the "divine Ariosto," a title which has never been popularly given to his rival.

The "Jerusalem Delivered" is the history of a Crusade related with poetic license. The Infidels are assisted by unlawful arts ; and the libertinism that brought scandal on the Christians is converted into youthful susceptibility, led away by enchantment. The author proposed to combine the ancient epic poets with Ariosto, or a simple plot and uniformly dignified style, with romantic varieties of adventure, and the luxuriance of fairy-land. He did what he proposed to do, but with a judgment inferior to

Virgil's; nay, in point of the interdependence of the adventures, to Ariosto and with far less general vigor. The mixture of affectation with his dignity is so frequent that, whether Boileau's famous line about Tasso's tinsel and Virgil's gold did or did not mean to imply that the "Jerusalem" was nothing but tinsel and the "Æneid" all gold, it is certain that the tinsel is so interwoven with the gold as to render it more of a rule than an exception, and put a provoking distance between Tasso's epic pretensions and those of the greatest masters of the art. People who take for granted the conceits because of the "wildness" of Ariosto, and the good taste because of the "regularity" of Tasso, just assume the reverse of the fact. It is a rare thing to find a conceit in Ariosto; and, where it does exist, it is most likely defensible on some Shakespearian ground of subtle propriety. Open Tasso in almost any part, particularly the love scenes, and it is marvellous if, before long, you do not see the conceits vexatiously interfering with the beauties.

"Oh, maraviglia! Amor, che appena è nato,
  Già grande vola, e già trionfa armato."—Canto i., st. 47.

O miracle! Love is scarce born, when, lo,
He flies full wing'd, and lords it with his bow!

"Se 'l miri fulminar ne l'arme avvolto,
  Marte lo stimi; Amor, se scopre il volto."—St. 58.

Mars you would think him when his thund'ring race
In arms he ran ; Love, when he show'd his face.

Which is as little true to reason as to taste ; for
no god of war could look like a god of love.
The habit of mind would render it impossible.
But the poet found the prettiness of the Greek
anthology irresistible.

Olindo, tied to the stake amidst the flames of
martyrdom, can say to his mistress :

"Altre fiamme, altri nodi amor promise."—Canto ii.,
st. 34.

Other flames, other bonds than these, love promised.

The sentiment is natural, but the double use of
the "flames" on such an occasion miserable.

In the third canto the fair Amazon Clorinda
challenges her love to single combat.

"E di due morti in un punto lo sfida."—St. 23.

"And so at once she threatens to kill him twice."
—*Fairfax.*

That is to say, with her valor and beauty.

Another twofold employment of flame, with
an exclamation to secure our astonishment,
makes its appearance in the fourth canto :

"Oh miracol d'amor ! che le faville
Tragge del pianto, e i cor' ne l' acqua accende."—St. 76.

O miracle of love ! that draweth sparks
Of fire from tears, and kindlest hearts in water !

This puerile antithesis of *fire* and *water*, *fire*
and *ice*, *light* in *darkness*, *silence* in *speech*, together with such pretty turns as *wounding one's
self in wounding others*, and the worse sacrifice
of consistency and truth of feeling,—lovers
making long speeches on the least fitting occasions, and ladies retaining their rosy cheeks
in the midst of fears of death,—is to be met
with, more or less, throughout the poem.   I
have no doubt they were the proximate cause
of that general corruptiou of taste which was
afterwards completed by Marino, the acquaintance and ardent admirer of Tasso when a boy.
They have been laid to the charge of Petrarch ;
but, without entering into the question how far
and in what instances conceits may not be natural to lovers haunted, as Petrarch was, with
one idea, and seeing it in every thing they behold, what had the great epic poet to do with
the faults of the lyrical ?   And what is to be
said for his standing in need of the excuse of
bad example ?   Homer and Milton were in no
such want.   Virgil would not have copied the
tricks of Ovid.   There is an effeminaucy and
self-reflection in Tasso, analogous to his " Rinaldo," in the enchanted garden, where the
hero wore a looking-glass by his side, in which

he contemplated his sophisticated self, and the meretricious beauty of his enchantress.*

Agreeable to this tendency to weakness, the style of Tasso, when not supported by great occasions (and the occasion itself sometimes fails him), is too apt to fall into tameness and commonplace,—to want movement and picture; while at the same time, with singular defect of enjoyment, it does not possess the music which might be expected from a lyrical and voluptuous poet. Bernardo prophesied of his son that, however he might surpass him in other respects, he would never equal him in sweetness; and he seems to have judged him rightly. I have met with a passage in Torquato's prose writings (but I cannot lay my hands on it), in which he expresses a singular predilection for verses full of the same vowel. He seems, if I remember rightly, to have regarded it, not merely as a pleasing variety, which it is on occasion, but as a reigning principle. Voltaire (I think in his treatise on " Epic Poetry ") has noticed the multitude of *o*'s in the exordium of the "Jerusa-

---

* It is an extraordinary instance of a man's violating, in older life, the better critical principles of his youth,— that Tasso, in his " Discourses on Poetry," should have objected to a passage in Ariosto about sighs and tears as being a " conceit too lyrical" (though it was warranted by the subtleties of madness), and yet afterwards riot in the same conceits when wholly without warrant.

lem.'' This apparent negligence seems to have been intentional.

" Cantò l' armi pictòse e 'l capitanò
    Che 'l gran Sepòlcrò liberò di Cristò ;
  Mòltò egli òprò còl sennò e còn la manò,
    Mòltò sòfri nel glòriòsò acquistò ;
  E invan l' infernò a lui s' òppòse ; e invanò
    S' armò d' Asia e di Libia il pòpòl mistò ;
  Che il ciel gli diè favòre, e sòttò ai santi
  Segni ridusse i suòi còmpagni erranti."

The reader will not be surprised to find, that he who could thus confound monotony with music, and commence his greatest poem with it, is too often discordant in the rest of his versification. It has been thought that Milton might have taken from the Italians the grand musical account to which he turns a list of proper names, as in his enumerations of realms and deities ; but I have been surprised to find how little the most musical of languages appears to have suggested to its poets any thing of the sort. I am not aware of it, indeed, in any poets but our own. All others, from Homer, with his catalogue of leaders and ships, down to Metastasio himself, though he wrote for music, appear to have overlooked this opportunity of playing a voluntary of fine sounds, where they had no other theme on which to modulate.

Its inventor, as far as I am aware, is that great poet, Marlowe.*

There are faults of invention, as well as style in the "Jerusalem." The Talking Bird, or bird

* Δαρδανιων αυτ' ηρχεν, εὐς καις Αγχισαο,
Αινειας· τον ὑπ' Αγχιση τεκε δι Αφροδιτη
Ιδης εν κνημοισι, θεα βροτῳ εννηθεισα·
Ουκ οιος· ἁμα τῳγε δυω Αντηνορος υἱε,
Αρχιλοχος τ', Ακαμας τε, μαχης εν ειδοτε πασης.
—"Iliad " ii., 819.

It is curious that these five lines should abound as much in *a*'s as Tasso's first stanza does in *o*'s. Similar monotonies are strikingly observable in the nomenclatures of Virgil. See his most perfect poem, the "Georgics" :

" Omnià secum
Armentàrius 'Afer àgit, tectumque, Làremque,
'Armàque, 'Amyclæumque cànem, Cressàmque pharetràm."—Lib. iii., 343.

It is clear that Dante never thought of this point. See his Mangiadore, Sanvittore, Natan, Raban, etc. at the end of the twelfth canto of the "Paradiso." Yet in his time poetry was *recilalived* to music. So it was in Petrarch's, who was a lutenist, and who "tried " his verses, to see how they would go to the instrument. Yet Petrarch could allow himself to write such a quatrain as the following list of rivers :

" Non Tesin, Pò, Varo, Arno, Adige e Tebro,
Eufrate, Tigre, Nilo, Ermo, Indo e Gange,
Tana, Istro, Alfeo, Garrona è 'l mar che frange,
Rodano, Ibero, Ren, Senna, *Albia, Era, Ebro !* "

In Tasso's "Sette Giornate," to which Black thinks Milton indebted for his grand use of proper names, the following is the way in which the poet writes :

" Di Silvàni
Di Pàni, e d' Egipàni, e d' àltri errànti,
Ch' empier lè solitariè incultè selvè
D' antichè maravigliè ; e quell' accòltò
Esercitò di Baccò in òriente
Ond' egli vinse, e trionfò degl' Indi,
Tornandò glòriòsò ai Greci lidi,
Siccòm' faviòlòsò anticò gridò."

The most diversified passage of this kind (as far as I am

that sings with a human voice (canto iv., 13) is a piece of inverisimilitude, which the author, perhaps, thought justifiable by the speaking horses of the ancients. But the latter were moved supernaturally for the occasion, and for a very fine occasion. Tasso's bird is a mere born contradiction to nature and for no necessity. The vulgar idea of the devil with horns and a tail (though the retention of it argued a genius in Tasso very inferior to that of Milton) is defensible, I think, on the plea of the German critics, that malignity should be made a thing

aware) is Ariosto's list of his friends at the close of the "Orlando; and yet such writing as follows would seem to show that it was an accident:

"Iò veggiò il Fracastòrò, il Bevazzanò,
Trifòn Gabriel, e il Tassò più lòntanò;
Veggò Niccòlò Tiepoli, e còn essò
Niccòlò Amaniò in me affissar le ciglia;
Autòn Fulgòsò, ch' a vedermi appressò
Al litò mòstra gaudiò e maraviglia.
Il miò Valeriò e quel che là s' è messò
Fuòr de le dònne," etc.

Even Metastasio, who wrote expressly for singers, and often with exquisite modulation, especially in his songs, forgets himself when he comes to the names of his *dramatis personæ*,—"'Artàserse, 'Aràtbàno, 'Arbàce, Màndàne, Semirà, Megàbise,"—all in one play.

"Gran cose io temo. Il mio germàno 'Arbàce
Pàrte prià de l' aurorà. Il pàdre armàto
Incontro, e non mi pàrlà. 'Accusà il cielo
'Agitàto 'Artàserse, e m' àbbàndonà."—

Atto i., sc. 6.

I am far from intending to say that these reiterations are not sometimes allowable, nay, often beautiful and desirable. Alliteration itself may be rendered an exquisite instrument of music. I am only speaking of monotony or discord in the enumeration of proper names.

low and deformed; but as much cannot be said for the storehouse in heaven, where St. Michael's spear is kept with which he slew the dragon, and the trident which is used for making earthquakes (canto vii., st. 81). The tomb which supernaturally comes out of the ground, inscribed with the name and virtues of Sueno (canto viii., st. 39), is worthy only of a pantomime; and the wizard in robes, with beech-leaves on his head, who walks dry-shod on water, and superfluously helps the knights on their way to Armida's retirement (xiv., 33), is almost as ludicrous as the burlesque of the river-god in the "Voyage" of Bachaumont and Chapelle.

But let us not wonder, nevertheless, at the effect which the "Jerusalem" has had upon the world. It could not have had it without great nature and power. Rinaldo, in spite of his aberrations with Armida, knew the path to renown, and so did the poet. Tasso's epic, with all its faults, is a noble production, and justly considered one of the poems of the world. Each of those poems hit some one great point of universal attraction, at least in their respective countries; and among the givers of fame in others. Homer's poem is that of action; Dante's of passion; Virgil's, of judgment; Milton's, of religion; Spenser's, of poetry itself;

Ariosto's, of animal spirits (I do not mean as respects gayety only, but in strength and readiness of accord with the whole play of nature); Tasso looked round with an ultra-sensitive-temperament, and an ambition which required encouragement, and his poem is that of tenderness. Every thing inclines to this point in his circle, with the tremulousness of the needle. Love is its all in all, even to the design of the religious war which is to rescue the sepulchre of the God of Charity from the hands of the' unloving. His heroes are all in love, at least those on the right side ; his leader, Godfrey, notwithstanding his prudence, narrowly escapes the passion, and is full of a loving consideration ; his amazon, Clorinda, inspires the truest passion, and dies taking her lover's hand ; his Erminia is all love for an enemy ; his enchantress Armida falls from pretended love into real, and forsakes her religion for its sake. An old father (canto ix.) loses his five sons in battle, and dies on their dead bodies of a wound which he has provoked on purpose. Tancred cannot achieve the enterprise of the Enchanted Forest, because his dead mistress seems to come out of one of the trees. Olindo thinks it happiness to be martyred at the same stake with Sophronia. The reconciliation of Rinaldo with his enchantress takes place within a few stanzas of the close

of the poem, as if contesting its interest with
religion. The "Jerusalem Delivered," in short,
is the favorite epic of the young : all the lovers
in Europe have loved it. The French have for-
given the author his conceits for the sake of his
gallantry : he is the poet of the gondoliers ; and
Spenser, the most luxurious of his brethren,
plundered his bowers of bliss. Read Tasso's
poem by this gentle light of his genius, and you
pity him twenty-fold, and know not what excuse
to find for his jailer.

The stories translated in the present volume,
though including war and magic, are all love-
stories. They were not selected on that account.
They suggested themselves for selection, as containing most of the finest things in the poem.
They are conducted with great art, and the characters and affections happily varied. The first
("Olindo" and "Sophronia") is perhaps unique
for the hopelessness of its commencement (I
mean with regard to the lovers), and the perfect,
and at the same time quite probable, felicity of
the conclusion. There is no reason to believe
that the staid and devout Sophronia would have
loved her adorer at all, but for the circumstance
that first dooms them both to a shocking death,
and then sends them, with perfect warrant, from
the stake to the altar. Clorinda is an Amazon,
the idea of whom, as such, it is impossible for

us to separate from the very repulsive and un-feminine images ; yet, under the circumstances of the story, we call to mind in her behalf the possibility of a Joan of Arc's having loved and been beloved ; and her death is a surprising and most affecting variation upon that of Agri-can in Boiardo. Tasso's enchantress Armida is a variation of the Angelica of the same poet, combined with Ariosto's Alcina ; but her pas-sionate voluptuousness makes her quite a new character in regard to the one ; and she is as dif-ferent from the painted hag of the " Orlando " as youth, beauty, and patriotic intentions can make her. She is not very sentimental ; but all the passion in the world has sympathized with her ; and it was manly and honest in the poet not to let her Paganism and vehemence hinder him from doing justice to her claims as a human being and a deserted woman. Her fate is left in so pleasing a state of doubt, that we gladly avail ourselves of it to suppose her married to Rinal-do, and becoming the mother of a line of Chris-tian princes. I wish they had treated her poet half so well as she would infallibly have treated him herself.

But the singer of the Crusades can be strong as well as gentle. You discern in his battles and single combats the poet ambitious of re-nown, and the accomplished swordsman. The

duel of Tancred and Argantes, in which the
latter is slain, is as earnest and fiery writing
throughout as truth and passion could desire ;
that of Tancred and Clorinda is also very powerful as well as affecting ; and the whole siege of
Jerusalem is admirable for the strength of its
interest. Every body knows the grand verse
(not, however, quite original) that summons
the devils to council, "Chinama gli abitator,"
etc.; and the still grander, though less original
one, describing the desolations of time, "Giace
l' alta Cartago." The forest filled with super-
natural terrors by a magician, in order that the
Christians may not cut wood from it to make
their engines of war, is one of the happiest
pieces of invention in romance. It is founded
in as true human feeling as those of Ariosto,
and is made an admirable instrument for the
aggrandizement of the character of Rinaldo.
Godfrey's attestation of all time, and of the
host of heaven, when he addresses his army in
the first canto, is in the highest spirit of epic
magnificence. So is the appearance of the
celestial armies, together with that of the souls
of the slain Christian warriors, in the last canto,
where they issue forth in the air to assist the
entrance into the conquered city. The classical
poets are turned to great and frequent account
throughout the poem ; and yet the work has a

strong air of originality, partly owing to the
subject, partly to the abundance of love-scenes,
and to a certain compactness in the treatment
of the main story, notwithstanding the luxuriance of the episodes. The "Jerusalem Delivered" is stately, well-ordered, full of action and
character, sometimes sublime, always elegant,
and very interesting—more so, I think, as a
whole, and in a popular sense, than any other
story in verse, not excepting the "Odyssey."
For the exquisite domestic attractiveness of the
second Homeric poem is injured, like the hero
himself, by too many diversions from the main
point. There is an interest, it is true, in that
very delay; but we become too much used to
the disappointment. In the epic of Tasso the
reader constantly desires to learn how the
success of the enterprise is to be brought about;
and he scarcely loses sight of any of the persons
but he wishes to see them again. Even in the
love-scenes, tender and absorbed as they are,
we feel that the heroes are fighters, or going
to fight. When you are introduced to Armida
in the Bower of Bliss, it is by warriors who
come to take her lover away to battle.

One of the reasons why Tasso hurt the style
of his poem by a manner too lyrical was, that
notwithstanding its deficiency in sweetness, he
was one of the profusest lyrical writers of his

nation, and always having his feelings turned
in upon himself. I am not sufficiently acquainted with his odes and sonnets to speak
of them in the gross; but I may be allowed to
express my belief that they possess a great deal
of fancy and feeling. It has been wondered
how he could write so many, considering the
troubles he went through; but the experience
was the reason. The constant succession of
hopes, fears, wants, gratitudes, loves, and the
necessity of employing his imagination, accounts for all. Some of his sonnets, such as
those on the Countess of Scandiano's lip ("Quel
labbro," etc.); the one to Stigliano, concluding
with the affecting mention of himself and his
lost harp; that beginning

"Io veggio in ciela scintillarle stelle,"

recur to my mind oftener than any others except Dante's "Tanto gentile" and Filicaia's
"Lament on Italy"; and with the exception
of a few of the more famous odes of Petrarch,
and one or two of Filicaia's and Guidi's, I know
of none in Italian like several of Tasso's, including his fragment, "O del grand' Apennino,"
and the exquisite chorus on the *Golden Age*,
which struck a note in the hearts of the world.

His "Aminta," the chief pastoral poem of
Italy, though, with the exception of that ode,

not equal in passages to the "Faithful Shep-
herdess" (which is a Pan to it compared with a
beardless shepherd), is elegant, interesting, and
as superior to Guarini's more sophisticate yet
still beautiful "Pastor Fido" as a first thought
may be supposed to be to its emulator. The
objection of its being too elegant for shepherds
he anticipated and nullified by making Love
himself account for it in a charming prologue,
of which the god is the speaker :

" Queste selve oggi raggionar d' Amore
   S' udranno in nuova guisa ; e ben parassi,
   Che la mia Deità sia quì presente
   In se medesma, e non ne' suoi ministri.
   Spirerò nobil sensi à rozzi petti ;
   Raddolcirò nelle lor lingue il suono :
   Perchè, ovunque i' mi sia, io sono Amore
   Ne' pastori non men che negli eroi ;
   E la disagguaglianza de' soggetti,
   Come a me piace, agguaglio : e questa è pure
   Suprema gloria, e gran miracol mio,
   Render simili alle più dotti cetre
   Le rustiche sampogne."

   After new fashion shall these woods to-day
   Hear love discoursed ; and it shall well be seen
   That my divinity is present here
   In its own person, not its ministers.
   I will inbreathe my fancies in rude hearts ;
   I will refine and render dulcet sweet
   Their tongues ; because, wherever I may be
   Whether with rustic or heroic men,

There am I Love; and inequality,
As it may please me, do I equalize ;
And 'tis my crowning glory and great miracle
To make the rural pipe as eloquent
Even as the subtlest harp.

I ought not to speak of Tasso's other poetry, or of his prose, for I have read little of either; though, as they are not popular with his countrymen, a foreigner may be pardoned for thinking his classical tragedy, "Torrismondo," not attractive, his "Sette Giornate" (Seven Days of the Creation) still less so, and his platonical and critical discourses better filled with authorities than reasons.

Tasso was a lesser kind of Milton, enchanted by the sirens. We discern the weak parts of his character, more or less, in all his writings ; but we see also the irrepressible elegance and superiority of the mind, which, in spite of all weakness, was felt to tower above its age, and to draw to it the homage as well as the resentment of princes.

ARIOSTO:

CRITICAL NOTICE OF HIS LIFE AND GENIUS.

CRITICAL NOTICE OF ARIOSTO'S LIFE AND GENIUS.*

THE congenial spirits of Pulci and Boiardo may be said to have attained to their height in the person of Ariosto upon the principle of a transmigration of souls, or after the fashion of that hero in romance who was heir to the bodily strengths of all whom he conquered.

Lodovico Giovanni Ariosto was born on the 8th of September, 1474, in the fortress at Reggio, in Lombardy, and was the son of Niccolò

* The materials for this notice have been chiefly collected from the poet's own writings (rich in autobiographical intimation), and from his latest editor, Panizzi. I was unable to see this writer's principal authority, Baruffaldi, till I corrected the proofs and the press was waiting; otherwise I might have added two or three more particulars, not, however, of any great consequence. Panizzi is, as usual, copious and to the purpose, and has, for the first time I believe, critically proved the regularity and connectedness of Ariosto's plots, as well as the hollowness of the pretensions of the house of Este to be considered patrons of literature. It is only a pity that his " Life of Ariosto " is not better arranged. I have, of course, drawn my own conclusions respecting particulars, and sometimes have thought I had reason to differ with those who have preceded me, but not, I hope, with a presumption unbecoming a foreigner.

Ariosto, captain of that citadel (as Boiardo had been), and Daria Maleguzzi, whose family still exists. The race was transplanted from Bologna in the century previous, when Obizzo the Third of Este, Marquess of Ferrara, married a lady belonging to it, whose Christian name was Lippa. Niccolò Ariosto, besides holding the same office as Boiardo had done at Modena as well as at Reggio, was master of the household to his two successive patrons, the Dukes Borso and Ercole. He was also employed, like him, in diplomacy, and was made a count by the Emperor Frederick the Third, though not, it seems, with remainder to his heirs.

Lodovico was the eldest of ten children, five sons and five daughters. During his boyhood theatrical entertainments were in great vogue at court, as we have seen in the life of Boiardo, and at the age of twelve, a year after the decease of that poet (who must have been well known to him, and probably encouraged his attempts), his successor is understood to have dramatized, after his infant fashion, the story of "Pyramus and Thisbe," and to have got his brothers and sisters to perform it. Panizzi doubts the possibility of these precocious private theatricals; but considering what is called "writing" on the part of children, and that only one other performer was required in the piece, or at best a third for the lion (which some little brother might have "roared like any sucking-dove"), I cannot see good reason for disbelieving the story. Pope was not twelve years old when he turned the siege of Troy into a play, and got his school-fellows to perform it, the part of Ajax being given to the gardener. Man is a theatrical animal (ζῷον μιμητικόν), and the instinct is developed at a very early period, as almost every family can witness that has taken its children to the "playhouse."

At fifteen the young poet, like so many others of his class, was consigned to the study of the law, and took a great dislike to it. The extreme nobility of his nature, and the wish to please his father, appear to have made him enter on it willingly enough in the first instance ; * but as soon as he betrayed symptoms of disgust, Niccolò, whose affairs were in a bad way, drove him back to it with a vehemence which must have made bad worse.† At the ex-

---

* See in his Latin poems the lines beginning :
   "Hæc me verbosas suasit perdiscere leges."
                       —"De Diversis Amoribus."
†"Mio padre mi cacciò con spiedi e lancie," etc.
                       —"Satira," vi.
There is some appearance of contradiction in this passage and the one referred to in the preceding note; but I think the conclusion in the text the probable one, and that he was not compelled to study the law in the first instance. He speaks more than once of his father's memory with great tenderness, particularly in the lines on his death entitled "De Nicolao Areosto."

piration of five years he was allowed to give it up.

There is reason to believe that Ariosto was "theatricalizing" during no little portion of this time, for in his nineteenth year he is understood to have been taken by Duke Ercole to Pavia and to Milan, either as a writer or performer of comedies, probably both, since the courtiers and ducal family themselves occasionally appeared on the stage, and one of the poet's brothers mentions his having frequently seen him dressed in character.*

On being delivered from the study of the law, the young poet appears to have led a cheerful and unrestrained life for the next four or five years. He wrote, or began to write, the comedy of the "Cassaria," probably meditated some poem in the style of Boiardo, then in the height of his fame, and he cultivated the Latin language, and intended to learn Greek, but delayed, and unfortunately missed it in consequence of losing his tutor. Some of his happiest days were passed at a villa, still possessed by the Maleguzzi family, called La Mauriziana, two miles from Reggio. Twenty-five years afterwards he called to mind, with sighs, the pleasant spots there which used to invite him

---

* His brother Gabriel expressly mentions it in his prologue to the "Scholastica."

to write verses; the garden, the little river, the mill, the trees by the water-side, and all the other shady places in which he enjoyed himself during that sweet season of his life "betwixt April and May."* To complete his happiness, he had a friend and cousin, Pandolfo Ariosto, who loved every thing that he loved, and for whom he augured a brilliant reputation.

But a dismal cloud was approaching. In his twenty-first year he lost his father, and found a large family left on his hands in narrow circumstances. The charge was at first so heavy, especially when aggravated by the death of Pandolfo, that he tells us he wished to die. He took to it manfully, however, in spite of these fits of gloom, and he lived to see his admirable efforts rewarded; his brothers enabled to seek their fortunes, and his sisters properly taken care of. Two of them, it seems, had become nuns. A third married; and a fourth remained long in his house. It is not known what became of the fifth.

In these family matters the anxious son and brother was occupied for three or four years, not, however, without recreating himself with his verses, Latin and Italian, and recording his admiration of a number of goddesses of his youth. He mentions, in particular, one of the

* "Già mi fur dolci inviti," etc.—"Satira," v.

name of Lydia, who kept him often from "his
dear mother and household," and who is probably represented by the princess of the same
name in the "Orlando," punished in the smoke
of Tartarus for being a jilt and coquette.* His
friend Bembo, afterwards the celebrated cardinal, recommended him to be blind to such little immaterial points as ladies' infidelities. But
he is shocked at the advice. He was far more of
Othello's opinion than Congreve's in such matters, and declared that he would not have
shared his mistress' good-will with Jupiter
himself.†

Towards the year 1504 the poet entered the
service of the unworthy prince, Cardinal Ippolito of Este, brother of the new Duke of
Ferrara, Alfonso the First. His eminence, who
had been made a prince of the church at thirteen years of age by the infamous Alexander
the Sixth (Borgia), was at this period little
more than one-and-twenty; but he took an
active part in the duke's affairs, both civil and
military, and is said to have made himself conspicuous in his father's lifetime for his vices
and brutality. He is charged with having

* See the beginning of "Astofo's Journey to the Moon."
† "Me potius fugiat, nullis mollita querelis,
    Dum simulet reliquos Lydia dura procos.
  Parte carere omni malo, quam admittere quemquam
  In Partem. Cupiat Juppiter ipse, negem."
                "Ad Petrum Benbum."

ordered a papal messenger to be severely beaten for bringing him some unpleasant despatches, which so exasperated his unfortunate parent that he was exiled to Mantua, and the marquess of that city, his brother-in-law, was obliged to come to Ferrara to obtain his pardon. But this was a trifle compared with what he is accused of having done to one of his brothers. A female of their acquaintance, in answer to a speech made her by the reverend gallant, had been so unlucky as to say that she preferred his brother Giulio's eyes to his eminence's whole body; upon which the monstrous villain hired two ruffians to put out his brother's eyes—some say, was present at the attempt. Attempt only it fortunately turned out to be,—at least in part, the opinion being that the sight of one of the eyes was preserved.*

Party spirit has so much to do with stories of princes, and the princes are so little in a condition to notice them, that, on the principle of not condemning a man till he has been heard in his defense, an honest biographer would be

---

* Panizzi, on the authority of Guicciardini and others. Giulio and another brother (Ferrante) afterwards conspired against Alfonso and Ippolito, and, on the failure of their enterprise, were sentenced to be imprisoned for life. Ferrante died in confinement at the expiration of thirty-four years; Giulio, at the end of fifty-three, was pardoned. He came out of prison on horseback, dressed according to the fashion of the time when he was arrested, and " greatly excited the curiosity of the people." —*Idem*, vol i., p. 12.

loath to credit these horrors of Cardinal Ippolito, did not the violent nature of the times, and
the general character of the man, even with
his defenders, incline him to do so. His being
a soldier rather than a churchman was a fault
of the age, perhaps a credit to the man, for he
appears to have had abilities for war, and it was
no crime of his if he was put into the church
when a boy. But his conduct to Ariosto showed
him coarse and selfish ; and those who say all
they can for him admit that he was proud
and revengeful, and that nobody regretted him
when he died. He is said to have had a taste
for mathematics, as his brother had for me-
chanics. The truth seems to be, that he and
the duke, who lived in troubled times, and had
to exert all their strength to hinder Ferrara
from becoming a prey to the court of Rome,
were clever, harsh men, of no grace or elevation of character, and with no taste but for war;
and if it had not been for their connection with
Ariosto, nobody would have heard of them, except while perusing the annals of the time. Ippolito might have been, and probably was, the
ruffian which the anecdote of his brother Giulio
represents him ; but the world would have
heard little of the villany, had he not treated a
poet with contempt.

The admirers of our author may wonder how

he could become the servant of such a man,
much more how he could praise him as he did
in the great work which he was soon to begin
writing. But Ariosto was the son of a man who
had passed his life in the service of the family ;
he had probably been taught a loyal blindness
to its defects ; gratuitous panegyrics of princes
had been the fashion of men of letters since the
time of Augustus, and the poet wanted help for
his relatives, and was of a nature to take the
least show of favor for a virtue till he had
learnt, as he unfortunately did, to be disappointed in the substance. It is not known
what his appointment was under the cardinal.
Probably he was a kind of gentleman of all
work ; an officer in his guards, a companion to
amuse, and a confidential agent for the transac-
tion of business. The employment in which he
is chiefly seen is that of an envoy, but he is said
also to have been in the field of battle ; and he
intimates in his " Satires " that household attentions were expected of him which he was
not quick to offer, such as pulling off his eminence's boots, and putting on his spurs.* It is
certain that he was employed in very delicate
negotiations, sometimes to the risk of his life

* "Che debbo fare io qui ?
   Agli usatti, agli spron (perch' io son grande)
   Non mi posso adattar, per porne o trarne."
                              " Satira," ii.

from the perils of roads and torrents. Ippolito, who was a man of no delicacy, probably made use of him on every occasion that required address, the smallest as well as greatest,—an interview with a pope one day, and a despatch to a dog fancier the next.

His great poem, however, proceeded. It was probably begun before he entered the cardinal's service ; certainly was in progress during the early part of his engagement. This appears from a letter written to Ippolito by his sister, the Marchioness of Mantua, to whom he had sent Ariosto at the beginning of the year 1509 to congratulate her on the birth of a child. She gives her brother special thanks for sending his message to her by "Messer Ludovico Ariosto," who had made her, she says, pass two delightful days, with giving her an account of the poem he was writing.* Isabella was the name of this princess ; and the grateful poet did not forget to embalm it in his verse.†

* " Per la lettera de la S. V. Reverendiss. et a bocha da Ms. Ludovico Ariosto ho inteso quanta leticia ha conceputa del felice perto mio : il che mi é stato summamente grato, cussi lo ringrazio de la visitazione, et particolarmente di havermi mandato il dicto Ms. Ludovico, per che ultra che mi sia stato acetto, representando la persona de la S. V. Reverendiss. lui anche per conto suo mi ha addutta gran satisfazione, havendomi cum la narratione de l' opera che compone facto passar questi due giorni non solum senza fastidio, ma cum piacer grandissimo."—Tiraboschi, "Storia della Poesia Italiana," Matthias' edition, vol. iii., p. 197.
† "Orlando Furioso," canto xxix., st. 29.

Ariosto's latest biographer, Panizzi, thinks he never served under any other leader than the cardinal; but I cannot help being of opinion with a former one, whom he quotes, that he once took arms under a captain of the name of Pio, probably a kinsman of his friend Alberto Pio, to whom he addresses a Latin poem. It was probably on occasion of some early disgust with the cardinal; but I am at a loss to discover at what period of time. Perhaps, indeed, he had the cardinal's permission, both to quit his service, and return to it. Possibly he was not to quit it at all, except according to events; but merely had leave given him to join a party in arms who were furthering Ippolito's own objects. Italy was full of captains in arms and conflicting interests. The poet might even, at some period of his life, have headed a troop under another cardinal, his friend Giovanni de' Medici, afterwards Leo the Tenth. He had certainly been with him in various parts of Italy, and might have taken part in some of his bloodless, if not his most military, equitations.

Be this as it may, it is understood that Ariosto was present at the repulse given to the Venetians by Ippolito when they came up the River Po against Ferrara towards the close of the year 1509, though he was away from the scene of action at the subsequent capture of their flotilla, the poet having been despatched between the two events to Pope Julius the Second on the delicate business of at once appeasing his anger with the duke for resisting his allies, and requesting his help to a feudatary of the church. Julius was in one of his towering passions at first, but gave way before the address of the envoy, and did what he desired. But Ariosto's success in this mission was nearly being the death of him in another, for Alfonso having accompanied the French, the year following, in their attack on Vicenza, where they committed cruelties of the same horrible kind as have shocked Europe within a few months past,* the poet's tongue, it was thought might be equally efficacious a second time; but Julius, worn out of patience with his too independent vassal, who maintained an alliance with the French when the pope had ceased to desire it, was to be appeased no longer. He excommunicated Alfonso, and threatened to pitch his envoy into the Tiber; so that the poet was fain to run for it, as the duke himself was afterwards, when he visited Rome to be absolved. Would Julius have thus treated Ariosto, could he have foreseen his renown? Probably he would. The greater the opposition to the will, the

*See the horrible account of the suffocated Vicentine Grottoes, in Sismondi, "Histoire des Republiques Italiennes," etc., vol. iv., p. 48.

greater the will itself. To chuck an accomplished envoy into the river would have been much; but to chuck the immortal poet there, laurels and all, in the teeth of the amazement of posterity, would have been a temptation irresistible.

It was on this occasion that Ariosto, probably from inability to choose his times or modes of returning home, contracted a cough, which is understood to have shortened his existence; so that Julius may have killed him after all. But the pope had a worse enemy in his own bosom —his violence—which killed him in a much shorter period. He died in little more than two years afterwards; and the poet's prospects were all now of a very different sort—at least he thought so; for in March, 1513, his friend Giovanni de' Medici succeeded to the papacy, under the title of Leo the Tenth.

Ariosto hastened to Rome, among a shoal of visitors to congratulate the new pope, perhaps not without a commission from Alfonso to see what he could do for his native country, on which the rival Medici family never ceased to have designs. The poet was full of hope, for he had known Leo under various fortunes; had been styled by him not only a friend, but a brother; and promised all sorts of participations of his prosperity. Not one of them came.

The visitor was cordially received. Leo stooped from his throne, squeezed his hand, and kissed him on both his cheeks ; but "at night," says Ariosto, "I went all the way to the Sheep to get my supper, wet through." All that Leo gave him was a "bull," probably the one securing him the profits of his "Orlando" ; and the poet's friend Bibbiena—wit, cardinal, and kinsman of Berni—facilitated the bull, but the receiver discharged the fees. He did not get one penny by promise, pope, or friend.* He complains a little, but all in good humor ; and good-naturedly asks what he was to expect, when so many hungry kinsmen and partisans were to be served first. Well and wisely asked, too, and with a superiority to his fortunes which Leo and Bibbiena might have envied.

It is thought probable, however, that if the poet had been less a friend to the house of Este, Leo would have kept his word with him, for their intimacy had undoubtedly been of the most cordial description. But it is supposed

> * " Piegossi a me dalla beata sede ;
> La mano e poi le gote ambe mi prese,
> E il santo bacio in amendue mi diede.
>
> " Di mezza quella bolla anco cortese
> Mi fu, della quale ora il mio Bibbiena
> Espedito m' ha il resto alle mie spese.
>
> " Indi col seno e con la falda piena
> De speme, ma di pioggia molle e brutto,
> La notte andia sin al Montone a cena."
>
> " Satira," iv.

that Leo was afraid he should have a Ferrarese envoy constantly about him, had he detained Ariosto in Rome. The poet, however, it is admitted, was not a good hunter of preferment. He could not play the assenter, and bow and importune; and sovereigns, however friendly they may have been before their elevation, go the way of most princely flesh when they have attained it. They like to take out a man's gratitude beforehand, perhaps because they feel little security in it afterwards.

The elevation to the papacy of the cheerful and indulgent son of Lorenzo de' Medici, after the troublous reign of Julius, was hailed with delight by all Christendom, and nowhere more so than in the pope's native place, Florence. Ariosto went there to see the spectacles; and there, in the midst of them, he found himself robbed of his heart by the lady whom he afterwards married. Her name was Alessandra Benucci. She was the widow of one of the Strozzi family, whom he had known in Ferrara, and he had long admired her. The poet, who, like Petrarch and Boccaccio, has recorded the day on which he fell in love, which was that of St. John the Baptist (the showy saint-days of the south offer special temptations to that effect), dwells with minute fondness on the particulars of the lady's appearance. Her dress

was black silk, embroidered with two grape-
bearing vines intertwisted ; and "between her
serene forehead and the path that went dividing
in two her rich and golden tresses," was a sprig
of laurel in bud. Her observer, probably her
welcome if not yet accepted lover, beheld something very significant in this attire ; and a
mysterious poem, in which he records a device
of a black pen feathered with gold, which he
wore embroidered on a gown of his own has
been supposed to allude to it. As everybody is
tempted to make his guess on such occasions, I
take the pen to have been the black-haired poet
himself, and the golden feather the tresses of
the lady. Beautiful as he describes her, with a
face full of sweetness, and manners noble and
engaging, he speaks most of the charms of her
golden locks. The black gown could hardly
have implied her widowhood ; the allusion
would not have been delicate. The vine belongs to dramatic poets, among whom the lover
was at that time to be classed, the "Orlando"
not having appeared. Its duplification intimated another self ; and the crowning laurel
was the success that awaited the heroic poet
and the conqueror of the lady's heart.*

* See *canzone* the first, " Non so s'io potrò," etc. ; and
the *capitolo* beginning " Della mi negra penna in fregio
d' oro."

The marriage was never acknowledged. The husband was in the receipt of profits arising from church-offices, which put him into the condition of the fellow of a college with us, who cannot marry so long as he retains his fellowship ; but it is proved to have taken place, though the date of it is uncertain. Ariosto, in a satire written three or four years after his falling in love, says he never intends either to marry or to take orders ; because, if he takes orders, he cannot marry ; and if he marries, he cannot take orders—that is to say, must give up his semi-priestly emoluments. This is one of the falsehoods which the Roman Catholic religion thinks itself warranted in tempting honest men to fall into ; thus perplexing their faith as to the very roots of all faith, and tending to maintain a sensual hypocrisy, which can do no good to the strongest minds, and must terribly injure the weak.

Ariosto's love for this lady I take to have been one of the causes of dissatisfaction between him and the cardinal. "Fortunately for the poet," as Panizzi observes, Ippolito was not always in Ferrara. He travelled in Italy, and he had an archbishopric in Hungary, the tenure of which compelled occasional residence. His company was not desired in Rome, so that he was seldom there. Ariosto, however, was an amusing companion; and the cardinal seems not to have liked to go anywhere without him. In the year 1515 he was attended by the poet part of the way on a journey to Rome and Urbino; but Ariosto fell ill, and had leave to return. He confesses that his illness was owing to an anxiety of love; and he even makes an appeal to the cardinal's experience of such feelings; so that it might seem he was not afraid of Ippolito's displeasure in that direction. But the weakness which selfish people excuse in themselves becomes a "very different thing" (as they phrase it) in another. The appeal to the cardinal's experience might only have exasperated him, in its assumption of the identity of the case. However, the poet was, at all events, left this time to the indulgence of his love and his poetry; and in the course of the ensuing year a copy of the first edition of the "Orlando Furioso," in forty cantos, was put into the hands of the illustrious person to whom it was dedicated.

The words in which the cardinal was pleased to express himself on this occasion have become memorable. "Where the devil, Master Lodovick," said the reverend personage, "have you picked up such a parcel of trumpery?" The original term is much stronger, aggravating the insult with indecency. There is no equivalent for it in English; and I shall not repeat it in Italian. "It is as low and indecent," says Panizzi, "as any in the language." Suffice it to say that, although the age was not scrupulous in such matters, it was one of the last words befitting the lips of the reverend Catholic; and that, when Ippolito of Este (as Ginguéné observes) made that speech to the great poet, "he uttered—prince, cardinal, and mathematician as he was—an impertinence." *

Was the cardinal put out of temper by a device which appeared in this book? On the leaf succeeding the title-page was the privilege for its publication, granted by Leo in terms of the most flattering personal recognition.† So far so good; unless the unpoetical Este patron was not pleased to see such interest taken in the book by the tasteful Medici patron. But on the back of this leaf was a device of a hive, with the bees burnt out of it for their honey,

---

* "Histoire Littéraire," etc., vol. iv., p. 335.

† "Singularis tua et pervetus erga nos familiamque nostrum observantia, egregiaque bonarum artium et litterarum doctrina, atque in studiis mitioribus, præsertimque poetices elegans et præclarum ingenium, jure prope suo a nobis exposcere videntur, ut quæ tibi usui futuræ sint, justa præsertim et honesta petenti, ea tibi liberaliter et gratiose concedamus. Quamobrem," etc. "On the same page," says Panizzi, "are mentioned the privileges granted by the king of France, by the republic of Venice, and other potentates"; so that authors, in those days, appear to have been thought worthy of

and their motto " Evil for good " (*Pro bono malum*). Most biographers are of opinion that this device was aimed at the cardinal's ill return for all the sweet words lavished on him and his house. If so, and supposing Ariosto to have presented the dedication copy in person, it would have been curious to see the faces of the two men while his eminence was looking at it. Some will think that the good-natured poet could hardly have taken such an occasion of displaying his resentment. But the device did not express at whom it was aimed ; the cardinal need not have applied it to himself if he did not choose, especially as the book was full of his praises ; and good-natured people will not always miss an opportunity of covertly inflicting a sting. The device, at all events, showed that the honey-maker had got worse than nothing by his honey ; and the house of Este could not say they had done any thing to contradict it.

I think it probable that neither the poet's de-

profiting by their labors, wherever they contributed to the enjoyment of mankind.

Leo's privilege is the one that so long underwent the singular obloquy of being a bull of excommunication against all who objected to the poem ! a misconception on the part of some ignorant man, or misrepresentation by some malignant one, which affords a remarkable warning against taking things on trust from one writer after another. Even Bayle (see the article " Leo X." in his Dictionary) suffered his inclinations to blind his vigilance.

vice nor the cardinal's speech were forgotten, when, in the course of the next year, the parties came to a rupture in consequence of the servant's refusing to attend his master into Hungary. Ariosto excused himself on account of the state of his health and of his family. He said that a cold climate did not agree with him ; that his chest was affected, and could not bear even the stoves of Hungary ; and that he could not, in common decency and humanity, leave his mother in her old age, especially as all the rest of the family were away but his youngest sister, whose interests he had also to take care of. But Ippolito was not to be appeased. The public have seen, in a late female biography, a deplorable instance of unfeelingness with which even a princess with a reputation for religion could treat the declining health and unwilling retirement of a poor slave in her service, fifty times her superior in every thing but servility. Greater delicacy was not to be expected of the military priest. The nobler the servant, the greater the desire to trample upon him and keep him at a disadvantage. It is a grudge which rank owes to genius, and which it can only waive when its possessor is himself " one of God Almighty's gentlemen." I do not mean in point of genius, which is by no means the highest thing in the world, whatever its owners may think of it; but in point of the highest of all things, which is nobleness of heart. I confess I think Ariosto was wrong in expecting what he did of a man he must have known so well, and in complaining so much of courts, however good-humoredly. A prince occupies the station he does, to avert the perils of disputed successions, and not to be what his birth cannot make him—if nature has not supplied the materials. Besides, the cardinal, in his quality of a mechanical-minded man with no taste, might with reason have complained of his servant's attending to poetry when it was "not in his bond;" when it diverted from the only attentions which his employer understood or desired. Ippolito candidly confessed, as Ariosto himself tells us, that he not only did not care for poetry, but never gave his attendant one stiver in patronage of it, or for any thing whatsoever but going his journeys and doing as he was bidden.* On the other hand, the cardinal's payments were sorry ones; and the poet might with justice have thought, that he was not bound to consider them an equivalent for the time he was expected to

---

* " Apollo, tua mercè, tua mercè santo
Collegio delle Muse, io non mi trovo
Tanto per voi, ch' io possa farmi un manto:

" E se 'l signor m' ha dato onde far novo,
Ogni anno mi potrei più d' un mantello,
Che mi abbia per voi dato, non approvo.
Egli l' ha detto."   " Satira," ii.

give up. The only thing to have been desired
in this case was, that he should have said so;
and, in truth, at the close of the explanation
which he gave on the subject to his friends at
court, he did—boldly desiring them, as became
him, to tell the cardinal, that if his eminence
expected him to be a "serf" for what he
received, he should decline the bargain;
and that he preferred the humblest freedom and his studies to a slavery so prepos-
terous.*

The truth is, the poet should have attached himself wholly to the Medici. Had he not adhered
to the duller house, he might have led as happy
a life with the pope as Pulci did with the pope's
father; perhaps have been made a cardinal,
like his friends Bembo and Sadolet. But then
we might have lost the "Orlando."

The only sinecure which the poet is now supposed to have retained, was a grant of twenty-
five crowns every four months on the episcopal
chancery of Milan: so, to help out his petty

---

* " Se avermi dato onde ogni quattro mesi
Ho venticinque scudi, nè sì fermi,
Che molte volte non mi sien contesi,

" Mi debbe incatenar, schiavo tenermi,
Obbligarmi ch' io sudi e tremi senza
Rispetto alcum, ch' io muoja o ch' io m' infermi,

" Non gli lasciate aver questa credenza:
Ditegli, che più tosto ch' esso servo,
Torrò la povertade in pazienza."   " Satira," ii.

income, he proceeded to enter into the service of Alfonso, which shows that both the brothers were not angry with him. He tells us that he would gladly have had no new master, could he have helped it ; but that, if he must needs serve, he would rather serve the master of every body else than a subordinate one. At this juncture he had a brief prospect of being as free as he wished ; for an uncle died leaving a large landed property still known as the Ariosto lands (*Le Arioste*); but a convent demanded it on the part of one of their brotherhood, who was a natural son of this gentleman ; and a more formidable and ultimately successful claim was advanced in a court of law by the Chamber of the Duchy of Ferrara, the first judge in the cause being the duke's own steward and a personal enemy of the poet's. Ariosto, therefore, while the suit was going on, was obliged to content himself with his fees from Milan and a monthly allowance which he received from the duke of "about thirty-eight shillings," together with provisions for three servants and two horses. He entered the duke's service in the spring of 1518, and remained in it for the rest of his life. But it was not so burdensome as that of the cardinal ; and the consequence of the poet's greater leisure was a second edition of the "Furioso," in the year 1521, with additions and corrections ; still, how-

ever, in forty cantos only. It appears, by a deed
of agreement,* that the work was printed at the
author's expense ; that he was to sell the bookseller one hundred copies for sixty livres (about
5*l.* 12*s.*) on condition of the book's not being
sold at the rate of more than sixteen sous (1*s.*
8*d.*); that the author was not to give, sell, or
allow to be sold, any copy of the book at Ferrara, except by the bookseller ; that the bookseller, after disposing of the hundred copies,
was to have as many more as he chose on the
same terms ; and that, on his failing to require
a further supply, Ariosto was to be at liberty to
sell his volumes to whom he pleased. " With
such profits," observed Panizzi, "it was not
likely that the poet would soon become independent " : and it may be added, that he certainly got nothing by the first edition, whatever
he may have done by the second. He expressly
tells us, in the satire which he wrote on declining to go abroad with Ippolito, that all his poetry had not procured him money enough to
purchase him a cloak.† Twenty years afterwards, when he was dead, the poem was in such
request, that, between 1542 and 1551, Panizzi
calculates there must have been a sale of it in

* Panizzi, vol. i., p. 29. The agreement itself is in Baruffaldi.

† See the lines before quoted, beginning " Apollo, tua
mercè."

Europe to the amount of a hundred thousand copies.*

The second edition of the "Furioso" did not extricate the author from very serious difficulties ; for the next year he was compelled to apply to Alfonso, either to relieve him from his necessities, or permit him to look for some employment more profitable than the ducal service. The answer of this prince, who was now rich, but had always been penurious,-and who never laid out a farthing, if he could help it, except in defence of his capital, was an appointment of Ariosto to the government of a district in a state of anarchy, called Garfagnana, which had nominally returned to his rule in consequence of the death of Leo, who had wrested it from him. It was a wild spot in the Apennines, on the borders of the Ferrarese and papal territories. Ariosto was there three years, and is said to have reduced it to order ; but, according to his own account, he had very doubtful work of it. The place was overrun with banditti, including the troops commissioned to suppress them. It required a severer governor than he was inclined to be ; and Alfonso did not attend to his requisitions for supplies. The candid and good-natured poet intimates that the duke

* "Bibliographical Notices of Editions of Ariosto," prefixed to his first vol., p. 51.

might have given him the appointment rather
for the governor's sake than the people's ; and
the cold, the loneliness and barrenness of the
place, and, above all, his absence from the object of his affections, oppressed him. He did
not write a verse for twelve months ; he says
he felt like a bird moulting.* The best thing,
got out of it was an anecdote for posterity. The
poet was riding out one day with a few attendants—some say walking out in a fit of absence
of mind—when he found himself in the midst
of a band of outlaws, who, in a suspicious manner, barely suffered him to pass. A reader of
Mrs. Radcliffe might suppose them a band of
condottieri, under the command of some profli-
gate desperado ; and such perhaps they were.
The governor had scarcely gone by, when the
leader of the band, discovering who he was,
came riding back with much earnestness, and
making his obeisance to the poet, said, that he
never should have allowed him to pass in that
manner had he known him to be the Signor
Lodovico Ariosto, author of the " Orlando Fu-

---

* " La novità del loco è stata tanta,
   C' ho fatto come augel che muta gabbia,
   Che molti giorni resta che non canta."

For the rest of the above particulars see the fifth satire,
beginning " Il vigesimo giorno di Febbraio." I quote
the exordium, because these compositions are differently
numbered in different editions. The one I generally use
is that of Molini—" Poesie Varie di Lodovico Ariosto,
con Annotazioni." Firenze, 12mo., 1824.

rioso ;" that his own name was Filippo Pacchi-
one (a celebrated personage of his order); and
that his men and himself, so far from doing the
signor displeasure, would have the honor of conducting him back to his castle. "And so they
did," says Baretti, "entertaining him all along
the way with the various excellences they had
discerned in his poem, and bestowing upon it
the most rapturous praises."*

On his return from Garfagnana, Ariosto is understood to have made several journeys in Italy,
either with or without the duke, his master;
some of them to Mantua, where it has been said
that he was crowned with laurel by the Emperor Charles the Fifth. But the truth seems to
be, that he only received a laureate diploma: it
does not appear that Charles made him any

---

* "Italian Library," p. 52. I quote Baretti, because
he speaks with a corresponding enthusiasm. He calls
the incident "a very rare proof of the irresistible powers
of poetry, and a noble comment on the fables of Orpheus
and Amphion," etc. The words "noble comment"
might lead us to fancy that Johnson had made some such
remark to him while relating the story in Bolt Court.
Nor is the former part of the sentence unlike him : "A
very rare proof, *sir*, of the irresistible powers of poetry,
and a noble comment," etc. Johnson, notwithstanding
his classical predilections, was likely to take much interest in Ariosto on account of his universality and the
heartiness of his passions. He had a secret regard for
"wildness" of all sorts, provided it came within any
pale of the sympathetic. He was also fond of romances
of chivalry. On one occasion he selected the history of
Felixmarte of Hyrcania as his course of reading during
a visit.

other gift. His majesty, and the whole house of Este, and the pope, and all the other Italian princes, left that to be done by the imperial general, the celebrated Alfonso Davallos, Marquess of Vasto, to whom he was sent on some mission by the Duke of Ferrara, and who settled on him an annuity of a hundred golden ducats; "the only reward," says Panizzi, "which we find to have been conferred on Ariosto expressly as a poet."* Davallos was one of the conquerors of Francis the First, young and handsome, and himself a writer of verses. The grateful poet accordingly availed himself of his benefactor's accomplishments to make him, in turn, a present of every virtue under the sun, Cæsar was not so liberal, Nestor so wise, Achilles so potent, Nireus so beautiful, nor even Ladas, Alexander's messenger, so swift.† Ariosto was now verging towards the grave ; and he probably saw in the hundred ducats a golden sunset of his cares.

Meantime, however, the poet had built a house, which, although small, was raised with

---

* The deed of gift sets forth the interest which it becomes princes and commanders to take in men of letters, particularly poets, as heralds of their fame, and consequently the special fitness of the illustrious and superexcellent poet Lodovico Ariosto for receiving from Alfonso Davallos, Marquess of Vasto, the irrevocable sum of, etc., etc. Panizza has copied the substance of it from Baruffaldi, vol. i., p. 67.

† "Orlando Furioso," canto xxxiii , st. 28.

his own money; so that the second edition of the "Orlando" may have realized some profits at last. He recorded the pleasant fact in an inscription over the door, which has become celebrated:

> " ' Parva, sed apta mihi; sed nulli obnoxia; sed non
> Sordida; parta meo sed tamen ære domus.''
>
> Small, yet it suits me; is of no offence;
> Was built, not meanly, at my own expense.

What a pity (to compare great things with small) that he had not as long a life before him to enjoy it, as Gil Blas had with his own comfortable quotation over his retreat at Lirias! *

The house still remains; but the inscription unfortunately became effaced; though the following one remains, which was added by his son Virginio:

> "Sic domus hæc Areostea
> Propitios habeat deos, olim ut Pindarica."
>
> Dear to the Gods, whatever come to pass,
> Be Ariosto's house, as Pindar's was.

This was an anticipation—perhaps the origin —of Milton's sonnet about his own house, ad-

---

* " Inveni portum: spes et fortuna, valete;
  Sat me lusistis; ludite nunc alios."
My port is found: adieu, ye freaks of chance;
The dance ye led me, now let others dance.

dressed to "Captains and Colonels," during the civil war.*

Davallos made the poet his generous present in the October of the year 1531; and in the same month of the year following the "Orlando" was published as it now stands, with various insertions throughout, chiefly stories, and six additional cantos. Cardinal Ippolito had been dead some time; and the device of the beehive was exchanged for one of two vipers, with a hand and pair of shears cutting out their tongues, and the motto, "Thou hast preferred ill-will to good" (*Dilexisti malitiam super benignatatem*). The allusion is understood to have been to certain critics whose names have all perished, unless Sperone (of whom we shall hear more by and by) was one of them. The appearance of this edition was eagerly looked for; but the trouble of correcting the press, and the destruction of a theatre by fire, which had been built under the poet's direction, did his health no good in its rapidly declining condition; and after suffering greatly from an obstruction, he died, much attenuated, on the sixth day of June, 1533. His decease, his fond biographers have told us, took place "about three in the afternoon"; and he was

* " The great Emathian conqueror bade spare
   The house of Pindarus, when temple and tower
   Went to the ground," etc.

"aged fifty eight years, eight months, and twenty-eight days." His body, according to his direction, was taken to the church of the Benedictines during the night by four men, with only two tapers, and in the most private and simple manner. The monks followed it to the grave out of respect, contrary to their usual custom.

So lived, and so died, and so desired humbly to be buried, one of the delights of the world.

His son Virginio had erected a chapel in the garden of the house built by his father, and he wished to have his body removed thither ; but the monks would not allow it. The tomb, at first a very humble one, was subsequently altered and enriched several times ; but remains, I believe, as rebuilt at the beginning of the century before last by his grand-nephew, Lodovico Ariosto, with a bust of the poet, and two statues representing Poetry and Glory.

Ariosto was tall and stout, with a dark complexion, bright black eyes, black and curling hair, aquiline nose, and shoulders broad but a little stooping. His aspect was thoughtful, and his gestures deliberate. Titian, besides painting his portrait, designed that which appeared in the woodcut of the author's own third edition of his poem, which has been copied into Mr. Panizzi's. It has all the look of truth of that great artist's vital hand ; but, though there is an expression of the genial character of the mouth, notwithstanding the exuberance of beard, it does not suggest the sweetness observable in one of the medals of Ariosto, a wax impression of which is now before me ; nor has the nose so much delicacy and grace.*

The poet's temperament inclined him to melancholy, but his intercourse was always cheerful. One biographer says he was strong and healthy—another, that he was neither. In all probability he was naturally strong, but weakened by a life full of emotion. He talks of growing old at forty-four, and of having been bald for some time.† He had a cough for many years before he died. His son says he cured it by drinking good old wine. Ariosto says that "vin fumoso" did not agree with him ; but that might only mean wine of a heady sort. The chances, under such circumstances, were probably against wine of any kind ; and Panizzi thinks the cough was never subdued. His phy-

---

* This medal is inscribed "Ludovicus Ariost. Poet." and has the bee-hive on the reverse, with the motto "Pro bono malum." Ariosto was so fond of this device that in his fragment called the "Five Cantos" (c. v. st. 26), the Paladin Rinaldo wears it embroidered on his mantle.

† " Io son de' dieci il primo, e vecchio fatto
  Di quaranta quattro anni, e il capo calvo
  Da un tempo in qua sotto il cuffiotto appiatto."
  "Satira," ii.

sicians forbade him all sorts of stimulants with his food.*

His temper and habits were those of a man wholly given up to love and poetry. In his youth he was volatile, and at no time without what is called some "affair of the heart." Every woman attracted him who had modesty and agreeableness; and as, at the same time, he was very jealous, one might imagine that his wife, who had a right to be equally so, would have led no easy life. But it is evident he could practise very generous self-denial; and probably the married portion of his existence, supposing Alessandra's sweet countenance not to have belied her, was happy on both sides. He was beloved by his family, which is never the case with the unamiable. Among his friends were most of the great names of the age, including a world of ladies, and the whole graceful court of Guidobaldo da Montefeltro, duke of Urbino, for which Catiglione wrote his book of the "Gentleman" (*Il Cartegiano*). Raphael ad-

---

* " Il vin fumoso, a me vie più interdetto
Che 'l tosco, costì a inviti si tracanna,
E sacrilegio è non ber molto, e schietto."

(He is speaking of the wines of Hungary, and of the hard drinking expected of strangers in that country.)

" Tutti li cibi son con pepe e canna,
Di amomo e d' altri aromati, che tutti
Come nocivi il medico mi danna."

" Satira," ii.

dressed him a sonnet, and Titian painted his likeness. He knew Vittoria Colonna, and Veronica da Gambera, and Giulia Gonzaga (whom the Turks would have run away with), and Ippolita Sforza, the beautiful blue-stocking, who set Bandello on writing his novels, and Bembo, and Flaminio, and Berni, and Molza, and Sannazzaro, and the Medici family, and Vida, and Macchiavelli; and nobody doubts that he might have shone at the court of Leo the brightest of the bright. But he thought it "better to enjoy a little in peace, than seek after much with trouble." * He cared for none of the pleasures of the great, except building, and that he was content to satisfy in Cowley's fashion, with "a small house in a large garden." He was plain in his diet, disliked ceremony, and was frequently absorbed in thought. His indignation was roused by mean and brutal vices; but he took a large and liberal view of human nature in general; and, if he was somewhat free in his life, must be pardoned for the custom of the times, for his charity to others, and for the genial disposition which made him an enchanting poet. Above all, he was an affectionate son; lived like a friend with his children; and, in spite of his tendency to pleasure, supplied the place of an anxious and

* Pigna, "I Romanzi," p. 119.

careful father to his brothers and sisters, who idolized him.

" Ornabat pietas et grata modestea vatem,"

wrote his brother Gabriel,

" Sancta fides, dictique memor, muniaque recto
　Justitia, et nullo patientia victa labore,
　Et constans virtus animi, et clementia mitis,
　Ambitione procul pulsa fastûsque tumore ;
　Credere uti posses natum felicibus horis,　＿
　Felici fulgente astro Jovis atque Diones." *

Devoted tenderness adorned the bard,
And grateful modesty and grave regard
To his least word, and justice arm'd with right,
And patience counting every labor light,
And constancy of soul, and meekness too,
That neither pride nor worldly wishes knew.
You might have thought him born when there concur
The sweet star and the strong, Venus and Jupiter.

His son Virginio, and others, have left a variety of anecdotes corroborating points in his character. I shall give them all for they put us into his company.

It is recorded, as an instance of his reputation for honesty, that an old kinsman, a clergyman, who was afraid of being poisoned for his possessions, would trust himself in no other hands : but the clergyman was his own grand-uncle

---

* *Epicedium* on his brother's death. It is reprinted (perhaps for the first time since 1582) in Mr. Panizzi's Appendix to the Life, in his first volume, p. clxi.

and namesake, probably godfather ; so that the compliment is not so very great.

In his youth he underwent a long rebuke one day from his father without saying a word, though a satisfactory answer was in his power ; on which his brother Gabriel expressing his surprise, he said that he was thinking all the time of a scene in a comedy he was writing, for which the paternal lecture afforded an excellent study.

He loved gardening better than he understood it ; was always shifting his plants, and destroying the seeds, out of impatience to see them germinate. He was rejoicing once on the coming up of some " capers," which he had been visiting every day to see how they got on, when it turned out that his capers were elder-trees !

He was perpetually altering his verses. His manuscripts are full of corrections. He wrote the exordium of the "Orlando" over and over again ; and at last could only be satisfied with it in proportion as it was not his own ; that is to say, in proportion as it came nearer to the beautiful passage in Dante from which his ear and his feelings had caught it.*

---

* " Le donne, i cavalier, l' arme, gli amori,
    Le cortesie, le audaci imprese, io canto,"
is Ariosto's commencement ;

    Ladies, and cavaliers, and loves, and arms,
    And courtesies, and daring deeds, I sing.

In Dante's " Purgatory " (canto xiv.), a noble Romagn-

He, however, discovered that correction was not always improvement. He used to say, it was with verses as with trees. A plant naturally well growing might be made perfect by a little delicate treatment; but over-cultivation destroyed its native grace. In like manner, you might perfect a happily-inspired verse by taking away any little fault of expression; but too great a polish deprived it of the charm of the first conception. It was like over-training a naturally graceful child. If it be wondered how he who corrected so much should succeed so well, even to an appearance of happy negligence, it is to be considered that the most impulsive writers often put down their thoughts too hastily, then correct, and re-correct them in the same impatient manner; and so have to bring them round, by as many steps, to the feeling which they really had at first, though they were too hasty to do it justice.

Ariosto would have altered his house as often as his verses, but did not find it so convenient. Somebody wondering that he contented himself with so small an abode, when he built such

ese, lamenting the degeneracy of his country, calls to mind with graceful and touching regret,

    " Le donne, i cavalier, gli affanni e gli agi,
     Che inspiravano amore e cortesia."

    The ladies and the knights, the cares and leisures,
    Breathing around them love and courtesy.

magnificent mansions in his poetry, he said it
was easier to put words together than blocks of
stone. *

He liked Virgil; commended the style of
Tibullus; did not care for Propertius; but expressed high approbation of Catullus and Hor-
ace. I suspect his favorite to have been Ovid.
His son says he did not study much, nor look
after books; but this may have been in his decline, or when Virginio first took to observing
him. A different conclusion as to study is to be
drawn from the corrected state of his manuscripts, and the variety of his knowledge; and
with regard to books, he not only mentions the
library of the Vatican as one of his greatest
temptations to visit Rome, but describes himself, with all the gusto of a book-worm, as enjoying them in his chimney-corner.†

To intimate his secrecy in love-matters, he
had an inkstand with a Cupid on it, holding a
finger on his lips. I believe it is still in existence.‡ He did not disclose his mistresses'

---

* The original is much pithier, but I cannot find equiva-
lents for the alliteration. He said, "Porvi le pietre e
porvi le parole non è il medesimo."—Pigna, p. 119.
According to his son, however, his remark was, that
"palaces could be made in poems without money." He
probably expressed the same thing in different ways to
different people.

† *Vide* "Sat.," iii. "Mi sia un tempo," etc.; and the
passage in "Sat.," vii., beginning "Di libri antiqui."

‡ The inkstand which Shelley saw at Ferrara ("Essays

names, as Dante did, for the purpose of treating them with contempt ; nor, on the other hand, does he appear to have been so indiscriminately gallant as to be fond of goitres. The only mistress of whom he complained he concealed in a Latin appellation ; and of her he did not complain with scorn. He had loved, besides Alessandra Benucci, a lady of the name of Ginevra ; the mother of one of his children is recorded as a certain Orsolina ; and that of the other was named Maria, and is understood to have been a governess in his father's family. *

He ate fast, and of whatever was next him, often beginning with the bread on the table before the dishes came ; and he would finish his dinner with another bit of bread. "Appetiva le rape," says his good son ; videlicet, he was fond of turnips. In his fourth Satire, he

and Letters," p. 149) could not have been this ; probably his eye was caught by a wrong one. Doubts also, after what we know of the tricks practised upon visitors of Stratford-upon-Avon, may unfortunately be entertained of the "plain old wooden piece of furniture," the armchair. Shelley describes the handwriting of Ariosto as "a small, firm, and pointed character, expressing, as he should say, a strong and keen, but circumscribed energy of mind." Every one of Shelley's words is always worth consideration ; but handwritings are surely equivocal testimonies of character ; they depend so much on education, on times and seasons and moods, conscious and unconscious wills, etc. What would be said by an autographist to the strange old, ungraceful, slovenly handwriting of Shakespeare?

* Baruffaldi, 1807, p. 105.

mentions as a favorite dish turnips seasoned with vinegar and boiled *must* (sapa), which seems, not unjustifiably, to startle Mr. Panizzi.* He cared so little for good eating, that he said of himself he should have done very well in the days when people lived on acorns. A stranger coming in one day at the dinner hour, he ate up what was provided for both, saying afterwards, when told of it, that the gentleman should have taken care of himself. This does not look very polite ; but of course it was said in jest. His son attributed this carelessness at table to absorption in his studies.

He carried this absence of mind so far, and at the same time was so good a pedestrian, that Virginio tells us he once walked all the way from Carpi to Ferrara in his slippers, owing to his having strolled out of doors in that direction.

The same biographers who describe him as a brave soldier, add that he was a timid horseman and seaman ; and indeed he appears to have eschewed every kind of unnecessary danger. It was a maxim of his to be the last in going out of a boat. I know not what Orlando would

* " In casa mia mi sa meglio una rapa
Ch' io cuoca, e cotta s' un stecco m' inforco,
E mondo, e spargo poi di aceto e sapa.

" Che all' altrui mensa tordo, starno, o porco Selvaggio."

have said to this, but there is no doubt that the
good son and brother avoided no pain in pursuit of his duty. He more than once risked
his life in the service of government from the
perils of travelling among war-makers and banditti. Imagination finds something worthy of
itself on great occasions, but is apt to discover
the absurdity of staking existence on small
ones. Ariosto did not care to travel out of Italy.
He preferred, he says going round the world in
a map; visiting countries without having to
pay innkeepers, and ploughing harmless seas
without thunder and lightning.*

His outward religion, like the one he ascribed
to his friend Cardinal Bembo, was " that of
other people." He did not think it of use to
disturb their belief; yet excused rather than
blamed Luther, attributing his heresy to the
necessary consequences of mooting points too
subtle for human apprehension.† He found it

---

* " Chi vuole andare," etc.
> " Satira," iv.

† " Se Nicoletto o Fra Martin fan segno
D' infedele o d' eretico, ne accuso
Il saper troppo, e men con lor mi sdegno :

" Perchè salendo lo intelletto in suso
Per veder Dio, non de' parerci strano
Se talor cade giù cieco e confuso."
> "Satira," vi.

This satire was addressed to Bembo. The cardinal is
said to have asked a visitor from Germany whether
Brother Martin really believed what he preached, and

impossible, however, to restrain his contempt
of bigotry; and like most great writers in Catholic countries, was a derider of the pretensions
of devotees and the discords and hypocrisies of
the convent. He evidently laughed at Dante's
figments about the other world; not at the
poetry of them, for that he admired, and sometimes imitated, but at the superstition and presumption. He turned the Florentine's moon
into a depository of nonsense; and found no
hell so bad as the hearts of tyrants. The only
other people he put into the infernal regions
are ladies who were cruel to their lovers! He
had a noble confidence in the intentions of his
Creator; and died in the expectation of meeting
his friends again in a higher state of existence.

Of Ariosto's four brothers, one became a cour-
tier at Naples, another a clergyman, another an
envoy to the Emperor Charles the Fifth, and
the fourth, who was a cripple and a scholar,
lived with Lodovico, and celebrated his memory. His two sons, whose names were Virginio

---

to have expressed the greatest astonishment when told
that he did. Cardinals were then what augurs were in
the time of Cicero—wondering that they did not burst
out a-laughing in one another's faces. This was bad;
but inquisitors are a million times worse. By the Nicoletto here mentioned by Ariosto in company with
Luther, we are to understand (according to the conjecture of Molini) a Paduan professor of the name of Nicolò
Vernia, who was accused of holding the Pantheistic
opinions of Averroes.

and Gianbattista, and who were illegitimate (the reader is always to bear in mind the more indulgent customs of Italy in matters of this nature, especially in the poet's time), became, the first a canon in the cathedral of Ferrara, and the other an officer in the army. It does not appear that he had any other children.

Ariosto's renown is wholly founded on the "Orlando Furioso," though he wrote satires, comedies, and a good deal of miscellaneous poetry, all occasionally exhibiting a master-hand. The comedies, however, were unfortunately modelled on those of the ancients ; and the constant termination of the verse with tri-syllables contributes to render them tedious. What comedies might he not have written had he given himself up to existing times and manners ! *

The satires are rather good-natured epistles to his friends, written with a charming ease and straightforwardness, and containing much

---

* Take a specimen of this leap-frog versification from the prologue to the "Cassaria":

"Questa commedia, ch' oggi *rscitàtavi*
Sarà, se nol sapete, è la *Cassària*,
Ch' un altra volta, già vent' anni *pàssano*,
Veder si fece sopra questi *pùlpiti*
Ed allora assai piacque a tutto il *pòpolo*,
Ma non ne ripostò già degno *prèmio*,
Che data in preda a gl' importuni ed *àvidi*
Stampator fu," etc.

This through five comedies in five acts !

exquisite sense and interesting autobiography. On his lyrical poetry he set little value; and his Latin verse is not of the best order. Critics have expressed their surprise at its inferiority to that of contemporaries inferior to him in genius; but the reason lay in the very circumstance. I mean that his large and liberal inspiration could only find its proper vent in his own language; he could not be content with potting up little delicacies in old-fashioned vessels.

The "Orlando Furioso" is literally a continuation of the "Orlando Innamorato"; so much so that the story is not thoroughly intelligible without it. This was probably the reason of a circumstance that would be otherwise unaccountable, and that was ridiculously charged against him as a proof of despairing envy by the despairing envy of Sperone; namely, his never having once mentioned the name of his predecessor. If Ariosto had despaired of equalling Boiardo, he must have been hopeless of reaching posterity, in which case his silence must have been useless; and in any case it is clear that he looked on himself as the continuator of another's narration. But Boiardo was so popular when he wrote that the very silence shows he must have thought the mention of his name superfluous. Still it is curious that he never should have alluded to it in the course of the poem. It could not have been from any dislike to the name itself, or the family; for in his Latin poems he has eulogized the hospitality of the house of Boiardo.*

The "Furioso" continued not only what Boiardo did, but what he intended to do ; for as its subject is Orlando's love and knight-errantry in general, so its object was to extol the house of Este, and deduce it from its fabulous ancestor Ruggiero. Orlando is the open, Ruggiero the covert hero ; and almost all the incidents of this supposed irregular poem, which, as Panizzi has shown, is one of the most regular in the world, go to crown with triumph and wedlock the originator of that unworthy race. This is done on the old groundwork of Charlemagne and his Paladins, of the treacheries of the house of Gan of Maganza, and of the wars of the Saracens against Christendom. Bradamante, the Amazonian *intended* of Ruggiero, is of the same race as Orlando, and a great overthrower of infidels. Ruggiero begins with being an infidel himself, and is kept from the wars, like a second Achilles, by the devices of an anxious guardian, but ultimately fights, is converted and marries ; and Orlando all the while slays his thousands, as of old, loves, goes mad for jealousy, is the foolishest and wisest of

* In the verses entitled " Bacchi Statua."

mankind (somewhat like the poet himself), and crowns the glory of Ruggiero not only by being present at his marriage, but putting on his spurs with his own hand when he goes forth to conclude the war by the death of the king of Algiers.

The great charm, however, of the "Orlando Furioso" is not in its knight-errantry, or its main plot, or the cunning interweavement of its minor ones, but in its endless variety, truth, force, and animal spirits ; in its fidelity to actual nature while it keeps within the bounds of the probable, and its no less enchanting verisimilitude during its wildest sallies of imagination. At one moment we are in the midst of flesh and blood like ourselves ; at the next with fairies and goblins ; at the next in a tremendous battle or tempest ; then in one of the loveliest of solitudes ; then hearing a tragedy, then a comedy ; then mystified in some enchanted palace ; then riding, dancing, dining, looking at pictures ; then again descending to the depths of the earth, or soaring to the moon, or seeing lovers in a glade, or witnessing the extravagancies of the great jealous hero Orlando ; and the music of an enchanting style perpetually attends us, and the sweet face of Angelica glances here and there like a bud ; and there are gallantries of all kinds, and stories endless, and honest tears, and joyous bursts of laughter, and beardings for all base opinions, and no bigotry, and reverence for whatsoever is venerable, and candor exquisite, and the happy interwoven names of "Angelica and Medoro," young forever.

But so great a work is not to be dismissed with a mere rhapsody of panegyric. Ariosto is inferior, in some remarkable respects, to his predecessors Pulci and Boiardo. His characters, for the most part, do not interest us as much as theirs by their variety and good fellowship ; he invented none as Boiardo did, with the exception, indeed, of Orlando's, as modified by jealousy ; and he has no passage, I think, equal in pathos to that of the struggle at Roncesvalles ; for though Orlando's jealousy is pathetic, as well as appalling, the effects of it are confined to one person, and disputed by his excessive strength. Ariosto has taken all tenderness out of Angelica, except that of a kind of boarding-school first love (which, however, as hereafter intimated, may have simplified and improved her general effect), and he has omitted all that was amusing in the character of Astolfo. Knight-errantry has fallen off a little in his hands from its first youthful and trusting freshness ; more sophisticate times are opening upon us ; and satire more frequently and bit-

terly interferes. The licentious passages (though
never gross in words, like those of his contemporaries) are not redeemed by sentiment as in
Boiardo ; and it seems to me that Ariosto hardly
improved so much as he might have done upon
his predecessor's imitations of the classics. I
cannot help thinking that, upon the whole, he
had better have left them alone, and depended
entirely on himself. Shelley says, he has too
much fighting and "revenge," *—which is true ;
but the revenge was only among his knights.
He was himself (like my admirable friend) one
of the most forgiving of men ; and the fighting
was the taste of the age, in which chivalry was
still flourishing in the shape of such men as
Bayard, and ferocity in men like Gaston de
Foix. Ariosto certainly did not anticipate, any
more than Shakespeare did, that spirit of human
amelioration which has ennobled the present
age. He thought only of reflecting nature as he
found it. He is sometimes even as uninteresting as he found other people ; but the tiresome
passages, thank God, all belong to the house of
Este ! His panegyrics of Ippolito and his ancestors recoiled on the poet with a retributive
dulness.

But in all the rest there is a wonderful in-
vigoration and enlargement. The genius of

* "Essays and Letters," *ut sup.*, vol. ii., p. 125.

romance has increased to an extraordinary degree in power, if not in simplicity. Its shoulders have grown broader, its voice louder and more sustained; and if it has lost a little on the sentimental side, it has gained prodigiously, not only in animal vigor, but, above all, in knowledge of human nature, and a brave and joyous candor in showing it. The poet takes a universal, an acute, and, upon the whole, a cheerful view, like the sun itself, of all which the sun looks on; and readers are charmed to see a knowledge at once so keen and so happy. Herein lies the secret of Ariosto's greatness; which is great, not because it has the intensity of Dante, or the incessant thought and passion of Shakespeare, or the dignified imagination of Milton, to all of whom he is far inferior in sustained excellence, but because he is like very Nature herself. Whether great, small, serious, pleasurable, or even indifferent, he still has the life, ease, and beauty of the operations of the daily planet. Even where he seems dull and commonplace, his brightness and originality at other times make it look like a good-natured condescension to our own common habits of thought and discourse; as though he did it but on purpose to leave nothing unsaid that could bring him within the category of ourselves. His charming manner intimates that, instead of taking thought, he chooses to take pleasure with us, and compare old notes ; and we are delighted that he does us so much honor, and makes, as it were, Ariostos of us all.   He is Shakespearian in going all lengths with Nature as he found her, not blinking the fact of evil, yet finding a "soul of goodness" in it, and, at the same time, never compromising the worth of noble and generous qualities.   His young and handsome Medoro is a pitiless slayer of his enemies ; but they were his master's enemies, and he would have lost his life, even to preserve his dead body.   His Orlando, for all his wisdom and greatness, runs mad for love of a coquette, who triumphs over warriors and kings, only to fall in love herself with an obscure lad. His kings laugh with all their hearts, like common people ; his mourners weep like such unaffected children of sorrow, that they must needs "swallow some of their tears." *   His heroes, on the arrival of intelligence that excites them, leap out of bed and write letters before they dress, from natural impatience, thinking nothing of their "dignity."   When

---

* " Le lacrime scendean tra gigli e rôse,
  Là dove avvien ch' alcune sè n' inghiozzi."
                                        Canto xii., st. 94.

Which has been well translated by Mr. Rose :

  " And between rose and lily, from her eyes
    Tears fall so fast, she needs must swallow some."

Astolfo blows the magic horn which drives everybody out of the castle of Atlantes, "not a mouse" stays behind—not, as Hoole and such critics think, because the poet is here writing ludicrously, but because he uses the same image seriously, to give an idea of desolation, as Shakespeare in "Hamlet" does to give that of silence, when "not a mouse is stirring." Instead of being mere comic writing, such incidents are in the highest epic taste of the meeting of extremes—of the impartial eye with which Nature regards high and low. So, give Ariosto his hippogriff, and other marvels with which he has enriched the stock of romance, and Nature takes as much care of the verisimilitude of their actions, as if she had made them herself. His hippogriff returns, like a common horse, to the stable to which he has been accustomed. His enchanter, who is gifted with the power of surviving decapitation and pursuing the decapitator so long as a fated hair remains on his head, turns deadly pale in the face when it is scalped, and falls lifeless from his horse. His truth, indeed, is so genuine, and at the same time his style is so unaffected, sometimes so familiar in its grace, and sets us so much at ease in his company, that the familiarity is in danger of bringing him into contempt with the inexperienced, and the truth of being considered old and obvious, because the mode of its introduction makes it seem an old acquaintance. When Voltaire was a young man, and (to Anglicize a favorite Gallic phrase) fancied he had *profounded* every thing deep and knowing, he thought nothing of Ariosto. Some years afterwards he took him for the first of grotesque writers, but nothing more. At last he pronounced him equally "entertaining and sublime, and humbly apologized for his error." Foscolo quotes this passage from the "Dictionnaire Philosophique"; and adds another from Sir Joshua Reynolds, in which the painter speaks of a similar inability on his own part, when young, to enjoy the perfect nature of Raphael, and the admiration and astonishment which, in his riper years, he grew to feel for it. *

The excessive "wildness" attributed to Ariosto is not wilder than many things in Homer, or even than some things in Virgil (such as the tranformation of ships into sea-nymphs). The reason why it has been thought so is, that he rendered them more popular by mixing them with satire, and thus brought them more universally into notice. One main secret of the delight they give us is their being poetical com-

* Essay on the " Narrative and Romantic Poems of the Italians," in the *Quarterly Review*, vol. xxi.

ments, at it were, on fancies and metaphors of
our own. Thus, we say of a suspicious man,
that he is suspicion itself; Ariosto turns him
accordingly into an actual being of that name.
We speak of the flights of the poets; Ariosto
makes them literally flights—flights on a hippogriff, and to the moon. The moon, it has
been said, makes lunatics; he accordingly puts
a man's wits into that planet. Vice deforms
beauty; therefore his beautiful enchantress
turns out to be an old hag. Ancient defeated
empires are sounds and emptiness; therefore
the Assyrian and Persian monarchies become,
in his limbo of vanities, a heap of positive bladders. Youth is headstrong, and kissing goes
by favor; so Angelica, queen of Cathay, and
beauty of the world, jilts warriors and kings,
and marries a common soldier.

And what a creature is this Angelica! what
effect has she not had upon the world in spite
of all her faults, nay, probably by very reason
of them! I know not whether it has been re-
marked before, but it appears to me, that the
charm which every body has felt in the story
of Angelica consists mainly in that very fact
of her being nothing but a beauty and a woman,
dashed even with coquetry, which renders her
so inferior in character to most heroines of
romance. Her interest is founded on nothing

exclusive or prejudiced. It is not addressed to
any special class. She might or might not
have been liked by this person or that; but
the world in general will adore her, because
nature has made them to adore beauty and the
sex, apart from prejudices right or wrong. Youth
will attribute virtues to her, whether she has
them or not; middle-age be unable to help
gazing on her; old-age dote on her. She is
womankind itself in form and substance; and
that is a stronger thing, for the most part, than
all our figments about it. Two musical names,
"Angelica and Medoro," have become identi-
fied in the minds of poetical readers with the
honeymoon of youthful passion.

The only false and insipid fiction I can call
to mind in the "Orlando Furioso" is that of
the "swans" who rescue "medals" from the
river of oblivion (canto xxxv.). It betrays a
singular forgetfulness of the poet's wonted
verisimilitude; for what metaphor can reconcile us to swans taking an interest in medals?
Popular belief had made them singers; but it
was not a wise step to convert them into anti-
quaries.

Ariosto's animal spirits, and the brilliant
hurry and abundance of incidents, blind a care-
less reader to his endless particular beauties,
which, though he may too often "describe in-

stead of paint" (on account, as Foscolo says, of his writing to the many), show that no man could paint better when he chose. The bosoms of his females "come and go, like the waves on the sea-coast in summer airs."* His witches draw the fish out of the water

"With simple words and a pure warbled spell."†

He borrows the word "painting" itself, like a true Italian and friend of Raphael and Titian, to express the commiseration in the faces of the blest for the sufferings of mortality:

"Dipinte di pietade il viso pio." ‡
Their pious looks painted with tenderness.

Jesus is very finely called, in the same passage, "il sempiterno Amante," the eternal Lover. The female sex are the

"Schiera gentil che pur adorna il mondo."§
The gentle bevy that adorns the world.

He paints cabinet pictures like Spenser, in isolated stanzas, with a pencil at once solid and light; as in the instance of the charming one that tells the story of Mercury and his net; how he watched the Goddess of Flowers as she

---

*"Vengono e van, come onda al primo margo
 Quando piacevole aura il mar combatte."
                                  Canto vii., st. 14.
†"Con semplici parole e puri incanti."
                                  Canto vi., st. 38.
‡ Canto xiv., st. 79.   § Canto xxviii., st. 98.

issued forth at dawn with her lap full of roses
and violets, and so threw the net over her
"one day," and "took her"';

"un dì lo presse."*

But he does not confine himself to these gentle pictures. He has many as strong as Michael
Angelo, some as intense as Dante. He paints
the conquest of America in five words:

"Veggio da diece cacciar mille." †

I see thousands
Hunted by tens.

He compares the noise of a tremendous battle
heard in the neighborhood to the sound of the
cataracts of the Nile:

"un alto suon ch' a quel s' accorda
Con che i vicin' cadendo il Nil assorda." ‡

He "scourges" ships at sea with tempests—
say rather the "miserable seamen"; while
nighttime grows blacker and blacker on the
"exasperated waters." ‖

When Rodomont has plunged into the thick
of Paris, and is carrying every thing before
him ("like a serpent that has newly cast his
skin, and goes shaking his three tongues under
his eyes of fire"), he makes this tremendous
hero break the middle of the palace-gate into

---

* Canto xv., st. 57.   † *Id.*, st. 23.
‡ Canto xvi., st. 56.   ‖ Canto xviii., st. 142.

a huge " window," and look through it with a countenance which is suddenly beheld by a crowd of faces as pale as death :

> " E dentro fatto l' ha tanta finestra,
> Che ben vedere e veduto esser puote
> Dai visi impressi di color di morte." *

The whole description of Orlando's jealousy and growing madness is Shakespearian for passion and circumstance ; and his sublimation of a suspicious king into suspicion itself (which it also contains) is as grandly and felicitously audacious as any thing ever invented by poet. Spenser thought so and has imitated and emulated it in one of his own finest passages. Ariosto has not the spleen and gall of Dante, and therefore his satire is not so tremendous ; yet it is very exquisite, as all the world have acknowledged in the instances of the lost things found in the moon, and the angel who finds Discord in a convent. He does not take things so much to heart as Chaucer. He has nothing so profoundly pathetic as our great poet's " Griselda." Yet many a gentle eye has moistened at the conclusion of the story of Isabella ; and to recur once more to Orlando's jealousy, all who have experienced that passion will feel it shake them. I have read somewhere of a visit

* Canto xvii., st. 12.

paid to Voltaire by an Italian gentleman, who recited it to him, and who (being moved perhaps by the recollection of some passage in his own history) had the tears all the while pouring down his cheeks.

Such is the poem which the gracious and good Cardinal Ippolito designated as a "parcel of trumpery." It had, indeed, to contend with more slights than his. Like all originals, it was obliged to wait for the death of the envious and self-loving, before it acquired a popularity which surpassed all precedent. Foscolo says, that Macchiavelli and Ariosto, "the two writers of that age who really possessed most excellence, were the least praised during their lives. Bembo was approached in a posture of adoration and fear ; the infamous Aretino extorted a fulsome letter of praises from the great and learned." * He might have added, that the writer most in request "in the circles " was a gentleman of the name of Bernardo Accolti, then called the *Unique*, now never heard of. Ariosto himself eulogized him among a shoal of writers, half of whose names have perished ; and who most likely included in that half the men who thought he did not praise them enough. For such was the fact ! I allude to the charming invention in his last canto, in

* " Essay," as above, p. 534.

which he supposes himself welcomed home after a long voyage. Gay imitated it very pleasantly in an address to Pope on the conclusion of his Homer. Some of the persons thus honored by Ariosto were vexed, it is said, at not being praised highly enough; others at seeing so many praised in their company; some at being left out of the list; and some others at being mentioned at all! These silly people thought it taking too great a liberty! The poor flies of a day did not know that a god had taken them in hand to give them wings for eternity. Happily for them the names of most of these mighty personages are not known. One or two, however, took care to make posterity laugh. Trissino, a very great man in his day, and the would-be restorer of the ancient epic, had the face in return for the poet's too honorable mention of him, to speak, in his own absurd verses, of "Ariosto," with that "Furioso of his, which pleases the vulgar":

"L'Ariosto
Con quel *Furioso* suo che piace al volgo."

"*His* poem," adds Panizzi, "has the merit of not having pleased any body."* A sullen critic, Sperone (the same that afterward plagued Tasso) was so disappointed at being left out, that he became the poet's bitter enemy. He

* "Boiardo and Ariosto," vol. iv., p. 318.

talked of Ariosto taking himself for a swan
and "dying like a goose" (the allusion was
to the fragment he left called the "Five Cantos"). What has become of the swan Sperone?
Bernardo Tasso, Torquato's father, made a
more reasonable (but which turned out to be
unfounded) complaint, that Ariosto had estab-
lished a precedent which poets would find inconvenient. And Macchiavelli, like the true
genius he was, expressed a good-natured and
flattering regret that his friend Ariosto had left
him out of his list of congratulators, in a work
which was "fine throughout," and in "some
places wonderful." *

The great Galileo knew Ariosto nearly by
heart. †

He is a poet whom it may require a certain
amount of animal spirits to relish thoroughly.
The *air* of his verse must agree with you before you can perceive all its freshness and
vitality. But if read with any thing like Italian
sympathy, with allowance for times and manners, and with a *sense* as well as *admittance* of
the different kinds of the beautiful in poetry
(two very different things), you will be almost
as much charmed with the "divine Ariosto"
as his countrymen have been for ages.

* "Life," in Panizzi, p. ix.
† "Opere di Galileo," Padova, 1744, vol. i., p. lxxii.

PULCI:

CRITICAL NOTICE OF HIS LIFE AND GENIUS.

CRITICAL NOTICE OF PULCI'S LIFE AND GENIUS.

PULCI, who was the first genuine romantic poet, in point of time, after Dante, seems, at first sight, in the juxtaposition, like farce after tragedy ; and indeed, in many parts of his poem, he is not only what he seems, but follows his saturnine countrymen with a peculiar propriety of contrast, much of his liveliest banter being directed against the absurdities of Dante's theology. But hasty and most erroneous would be the conclusion that he was nothing but a banterer. He was a true poet of the mixed order, grave as well as gay ; had a reflecting mind, a susceptible and most affectionate heart ; and perhaps was never more in earnest than when he gave vent to his dislike of bigotry in his most laughable sallies.

Luigi Pulci, son of Jacopo Pulci and Brigida de' Bardi, was of a noble family, so ancient as to be supposed to have come from France into

Tuscany with his hero Charlemagne. He was
born in Florence on the 3d of December, 1431,
and was the youngest of three brothers, all
possessed of a poetical vein, though it did not
flow with equal felicity. Bernardo, the eldest,
was the earliest translator of the Eclogues of
Virgil; and Lucca wrote a romance called the
"Ciriffo Calvaneo," and is commended for his
"Heroic Epistles." Little else is known of
these brothers; and not much more of Luigi
himself, except that he married a lady of the
name of Lucrezia degli Albizzi, journeyed in
Lombardy and elsewhere, was one of the most
intimate friends of Lorenzo de Medici and his
literary circle, and apparently led a life the
most delightful to a poet, always meditating
some composition, and buried in his woods and
gardens. Nothing is known of his latter days.
An unpublished work of little credit (Zilioli
"On the Italian Poets"), and an earlier printed
book, which, according to Tiraboschi, is of not
much greater (Scardeone "De Antiquitatibus
Urbis Patavinæ"), say that he died miserably
in Padua, and was refused Christian burial on
account of his impieties. It is not improbable
that, during the eclipse of the fortunes of the
Medici family, after the death of Lorenzo,
Pulci may have partaken of its troubles; and
there is certainly no knowing how badly his or

their enemies may have treated him ; but miserable ends are a favorite allegation with theological opponents. The Calvinists affirm of their master, the burner of Servetus, that he died like a saint ; but I have seen a biography in Italian which attributed the most horrible death-bed, not only to the atrocious Genevese, but to the genial Luther, calling them both the greatest villains (*sceleratissimi*), and adding that one of them (I forget which) was found dashed on the floor of his bedroom, and torn limb from limb.

Pulci appears to have been slender in person, with small eyes and a ruddy face. I gather this from the caricature of him in the poetical paper-war carried on between him and his friend Matteo Franco, a Florentine canon, which is understood to have been all in good humor—sport to amuse their friends—a perilous speculation. Besides his share in these verses, he is supposed to have had a hand in his brother's romance, and was certainly the author of some devout poems, and of a burlesque panegyric on a country damsel, "La Beca," in emulation of the charming poem "La Nencia," the first of its kind, written by that extraordinary person, his illustrious friend Lorenzo, who, in the midst of his cares and glories as the balancer of the power of Italy, was one of the liveliest of the native wits, and wrote songs for the people to dance to in Carnival time.

The intercourse between Lorenzo and Pulci was of the most familiar kind. Pulci was sixteen years older, but of a nature which makes no such differences felt between associates. He had known Lorenzo from the latter's youth, probably from his birth—is spoken of in a tone of domestic intimacy by his wife—and is enumerated by him among his companions in a very special and characteristic manner in his poem on Hawking ("La Caccia col Falcone"), when, calling his fellow-sportsmen about him, and missing Luigi, one of them says that he has strolled into a wood, to put something which has struck his fancy into a sonnet :

" 'Luigi Pulci ov' è, che non si sente?'
 'Egli se n' andò dianzi in quel boschetto,
Che qualche fantasia ha per la mente ;
 Vorr à fantasticar forse un sonetto.' "

" And where 's Luigi Pulci? I saw *him*."
 "Oh, in the wood there. Gone, depend upon it,
To vent some fancy in his brain—some whim,
 That will not let him rest till it 's a sonnet."

In a letter written to Lorenzo, when the future statesman, then in his seventeenth year, was making himself personally acquainted with the courts of Italy, Pulci speaks of himself as struggling hard to keep down the poetic pro-

pensity in his friend's absence. "If you were
with me," he says, "I should produce heaps
of sonnets as big as the clubs they make of the
cherry-blossoms for May-day. I am always
muttering some verse or other betwixt my
teeth; but I say to myself, 'My Lorenzo is not
here—he who is my only hope and refuge';
and so I suppress it." Such is the first, and of
a like nature are the latest accounts we possess
of the sequestered though companionable poet.
He preferred one congenial listener who understood him, to twenty critics that were puzzled
with the vivacity of his impulses. Most of the
learned men patronized by Lorenzo probably
quarrelled with him on account of it, plaguing
him in somewhat the same spirit, though in
more friendly guise, as the Della Cruscans and
others afterwards plagued Tasso; so he banters
them in turn, and takes refuge from their critical rules and commonplaces in the larger
indulgence of his friend Politian and the laughing wisdom of Lorenzo.

> "So che andar dirtito mi bisogna,
> Ch' io non ci mescolassi una bugia,
> Che questa non è storia da menzogna ;
> Che come io esco un passo de la via,
> Chi gracchia, chi riprende, e chi rampogna :
> Ognun poi mi riesce la pazzia ;
> Tanto ch' eletto ho solitaria vita,
> Che la turba di questi è infinita.

"La mia Accademia un tempo, o mia Ginnasia,
E stata volentier ne' miei boschetti ;
E puossi ben veder l' Affrica e l' Asia :
Vengon le Ninfe con lor canestretti,
E portanmi o narciso o colocasia ;
E così fuggo mille urban dispetti :
Sì ch' io non torno a' vostri Areopaghi,
Gente pur sempre di mal dicer vaghi."

I know I ought to make no dereliction
    From the straight path to this side or to that ;
I know the story I relate 's no fiction,
    And that the moment that I quit some flat,
Folks are all puff, and blame, and contradiction,
    And swear I never know what I 'd be at ;
In short, such crowds, I find, can mend one's poem,
I live retired, on purpose not to know 'em.

Yes, gentlemen, my only "Acàdeme,"
    My sole "Gymnasium," are my woods and bowers ;
Of Afric and of Asia there I dream ;
    And the Nymphs bring me baskets full of flowers,
Arums, and sweet narcissus from the stream ;
    And thus my Muse escapeth your town-hours
And town-disdains ; and I eschew your bites,
Judges of books, grim Areopagites.

He is here jesting, as Foscolo has observed, on the academy instituted by Lorenzo for encouraging the Greek language, doubtless with the laughing approbation of the founder, who was sometimes not a little troubled himself with the squabbles of his literati.

Our author probably had good reason to call his illustrious friend his "refuge." The "Mor-

gante Maggiore," the work which has rendered
the name of Pulci renowned, was an attempt
to elevate the popular and homely narrative-
poetry chanted in the streets into the dignity
of a production that should last. The age was
in a state of transition on all points. The dog-
matic authority of the schoolmen in matters of
religion, which prevailed in the time of Dante,
had come to nought before the advance of
knowledge in general and the indifference of
the court of Rome. The council of Trent, as
Crescimbeni advised the critics, had not then
settled what Christendom was to believe ; and
men, provided they complied with forms and
admitted certain main articles, were allowed to
think, and even in great measure talk, as they
pleased. The lovers of the Platonic philosophy took the opportunity of exalting some of
its dreams to an influence which at one time
was supposed to threaten Christianity itself,
and which in fact had already succeeded in affecting Christian theology to an extent which
the scorners of Paganism little suspect. Most
of these Helenists pushed their admiration of
Greek literature to an excess. They were opposed by the Virgilian predilections of Pulci's
friend, Politian, who had nevertheless universality enough to sympathize with the delight
the other took in their native Tuscan, and its

liveliest and most idiomatic effusions. From
all these circumstances in combination arose,
first, Pulci's determination to write a poem of a
mixed order, which should retain for him the
ear of the many, and at the same time give rise
to a poetry of romance worthy of higher auditors ; second, his banter of what he considered
unessential and injurious dogmas of belief, in
favor of those principles of the religion of
charity which inflict no contradiction on the
heart and understanding ; third, the trouble
which seems to have been given him by critics,
" sacred and profane," in consequence of these
originalities ; and lastly, a doubt which has
strangely existed with some, as to whether he
intended to write a serious or a comic poem, or
on any one point was in earnest at all. One
writer thinks he cannot have been in earnest,
because he opens every canto with some pious
invocation ; another asserts that the piety itself
is a banter ; a similar critic is of opinion that
to mix levities with gravities proves the gravities to have been nought, and the levities all in
all ; a fourth allows him to have been serious
in his description of the battle of Roncesvalles,
but says he was laughing in all the rest of his
poem ; while a fifth candidly gives up the question, as one of those puzzles occasioned by the
caprices of the human mind, which it is impos-

sible for reasonable people to solve. Even Sismondi, who was well acquainted with the age in which Pulci wrote, and who, if not a profound is generally an acute and liberal critic, confesses himself to be thus confounded: "Pulci," he says, commences all his cantos by a sacred invocation ; and the interests of religion are constantly intermingled with the adventures of his story in a manner capricious and little instructive. We know not how to reconcile this monkish spirit with the semipagan character of society under Lorenzo di Medici, nor whether we ought to accuse Pulci of gross bigotry or of profane derision."* Sismondi did not consider that the lively and impassioned people of the south take what may be called household liberties with the objects

* "Literature of the South of Europe," Thomas Roscoe's Translation, vol. II., p. 54. For the opinions of other writers, here and elsewhere alluded to, see Tiraboschi (who is quite frightened at him), "Storia della Poesia Italiana," cap. V., sec. 25 ; Gravina, who is more so, " Della Ragion Poetica " (quoted in Ginguéné, as below) ; Crescimbeni, "Commentari Intorno all' Istoria della Poesia," etc., lib. VI., cap. 3 (Matthias' edition), and the biographical additions to the same work, 4to, Rome, 1710, vol. II., part II., p. 151, where he says that Pulci was perhaps the " modestest and most temperate writer " of his age ("il più modesto e moderato ") ; Ginguéné, "Histoire Littéraire d'Italie," tom. IV., p. 214 ; Foscolo, in the *Quarterly Review*, as further on ; Panizzi on the " Romantic Poetry of the Italians," ditto ; Stebbing, " Lives of the Italian Poets," second edition, vol. I.; and the first volume of "Lives of Literary and Scientific men," in " Lardner's Cyclopædia."

of their worship greater than northerns can easily conceive; that levity of manner, therefore, does not always imply the absence of the gravest belief; that, be this as it may, the belief may be as grave on some points as light on others, perhaps the more so for that reason; and that although some poems, like some people, are altogether grave, or the reverse, there really is such a thing as tragi-comedy both in the world itself and in the representations of it. A jesting writer may be quite as much in earnest when he professes to be so, as a pleasant companion who feels for his own or for other people's misfortunes, and who is perhaps obliged to affect or resort to his very pleasantry sometimes, because he feels more acutely than the gravest. The sources of tears and smiles lie close to; aye, and help to refine one another. If Dante had been capable of more levity, he would have been guilty of less melancholy absurdities. If Rabelais had been able to weep as well as to laugh, and to love as well as to be licentious, he would have had faith and therefore support in something earnest, and not have been obliged to place the consummation of all things in the wine bottle. People's everyday experiences might explain to them the greatest apparent inconsistencies of Pulci's muse, if habit itself did not blind them to the

illustration. Was nobody ever present in a
well-ordered family, when a lively conversation
having been interrupted by the announcement
of dinner, the company, after listening with
the greatest seriousness to a grace delivered
with equal seriousness, perhaps by a clergyman, resumed it the instant afterwards in all
its gaiety, with the first spoonful of soup?
Well, the sacred invocations at the beginning
of Pulci's cantos were compliances of the like
sort with a custom. They were recited and
listened to just as gravely at Lorenzo di Medici's
table ; and yet neither compromised the recit-
ers nor were at all associated with the enjoyment of the fare that ensued. So with regard
to the intermixture of grave and gay throughout the poem. How many campaigning adventures have been written by gallant officers
whose animal spirits saw food for gaiety in half
the circumstances that occurred, and who could
crack a jest and a helmet perhaps with almost
equal vivacity, and yet be as serious as the
gravest at a moment's notice, mourn heartily
over the deaths of their friends, and shudder
with indignation and horror at the outrages
committed in a captured city? It is thus that
Pulci writes, full no less of feeling than
of whim and mirth. And the whole honest
round of humanity not only warrants his plan,

but in the twofold sense of the word embraces it.

If any thing more were necessary to show the gravity with which our author addressed himself to his subject, it is the fact, related by himself, of its having been recommended to him by Lorenzo's mother, Lucrezia Tornabuoni, a good and earnest woman, herself a poetess, who wrote a number of sacred narratives, and whose virtues he more than once records with the greatest respect and tenderness. The "Morgante" concludes with an address respecting this lady to the Virgin, and with a hope that her "devout and sincere" spirit may obtain peace for him in Paradise. These are the last words in the book. Is it credible that expressions of this kind, and employed on such an occasion, could have had no serious meaning? or that Lorenzo listened to such praises of his mother as to a jest?

I have no doubt that, making allowance for the age in which he lived, Pulci was an excellent Christian. His orthodoxy, it is true, was not the orthodoxy of the times of Dante or St. Dominic, nor yet of that of the Council of Trent. His opinions respecting the mystery of the Trinity appear to have been more like those of Sir Isaac Newton than of Archdeacon Travis. And assuredly he agreed with Origen respecting eternal punishment, rather than with Calvin and Mr. Toplady. But a man may accord with Newton, and yet be thought not unworthy of the "starry spheres." He may think, with Origen, that God intends all his creatures to be ultimately happy,* and yet be considered as loving a follower of Christ as a "dealer of damnation round the land," or the burner of a fellow-creature.

Pulci was in advance of his time on more subjects than one. He pronounced the existence of a new and inhabited world, before the appearance of Columbus.† He made the conclusion, doubtless, as Columbus did, from the speculations of more scientific men, and the rumors of seamen ; but how rare are the minds that are foremost to throw aside even the most innocent prejudices, and anticipate the enlargements of the public mind ! How many also are calumniated and persecuted for so doing, whose memories, for the same identical reason, are loved, perhaps adored, by the descendants of the calumniators ! In a public library, in Pulci's native place, is preserved a little withered relic, to which the attention of the visitor is drawn with reverential complacency. It stands, pointing upwards, under a glass-case, looking like a mysterious bit of parchment ; and is the

* Canto xxv. † *Idem*.

finger of Galileo ; of that Galileo, whose hand, possessing that finger, is supposed to have been tortured by the Inquisition for writing what every one now believes. He was certainly persecuted and imprisoned by the Inquisition. Milton saw and visited him under the restraint of that scientific body in his own house. Yet Galileo did more by his disclosures of the stars towards elevating our ideas of the Creator, than all the so-called saints and polemics that screamed at one another in the pulpits of East and West.

Like the "Commedia" of Dante, Pulci's "Commedia" (for such also in regard to its general cheerfulness,* and probably to its mediocrity of style, he calls it) is a representative in great measure of the feeling and knowledge of his time ; and though not entirely such in a learned and eclectic sense, and not to be compared to that sublime monstrosity in point of genius and power, is as superior to it in liberal opinion and in a certain pervading lovingness, as the author's affectionate disposition, and his country's advance in civilization, combined to render

---

* Canto xxvii., stanza 2.

       " S' altro ajuto qui non si dimostra,
    Sarà pur tragedía la istoria nostra.

      " Ed io pur commedía pensato avea
    Iscriver del mio Carlo finalmente,
   • Ed *Alcuin* così mi promettea," etc.

it. The editor of the " Parnaso Italiano " had reason to notice this engaging personal character in our author's work. He says, speaking of the principal romantic poets of Italy, that the reader will " admire Tasso, will adore Ariosto, but will love Pulci."* And all minds, in which lovingness produces love, will agree with him.

The " Morgante Maggiori " is a history of the fabulous exploits and death of Orlando, the great hero of Italian romance, and of the wars and calamities brought on his fellow Paladins and their sovereign Charlemagne by the envy, ambition, and treachery of the misguided monarch's favorite, Gan of Maganza (Mayence), Count of Poictiers. It is founded on the pseudo-history of Archbishop Turpin, which, though it received the formal sanction of the Church, is a manifest forgery, and became such a jest with the wits, that they took a delight in palming upon it their most incredible fictions. The title (" Morgante the Great ") seems to have been either a whim to draw attention to an old subject, or the result of an intention to do more with the giant so called than took place ; for though he is a conspicuous actor in the earlier part of the poem, he dies when it is not much

---

* " In fine tu adorerai l'Ariosto, tu ammirerei il Tasso, ma tu amerai il Pulci."—" Parn. Ital.," vol. ix., p. 344.

more than half completed. Orlando, the champion of the faith, is the real hero of it, and Gan the anti-hero or vice. Charlemagne, the reader hardly need be told, is represented, for the most part, as a very different person from what he appears in history. In truth, as Ellis and Panizzi have shown, he is either an exaggeration (still misrepresented) of Charles Martel, the Armorican chieftain, who conquered the Saracens at Poictiers, or a concretion of all the Charleses of the Carlovingian race, wise and simple, potent and weak.*

The story may be thus briefly told. Orlando quits the court of Charlemagne in disgust, but is always ready to return to it when the emperor needs his help. The best Paladins follow, to seek him. He meets with and converts the giant Morgante, whose aid he receives in many adventures, among which is the taking of Babylon. The other Paladins, his cousin Rinaldo especially, have their separate adventures, all more or less mixed up with the treacheries and thanklessness of Gan (for they assist even him), and the provoking trust reposed in him by Charlemagne ; and at length the villain crowns his infamy by luring Orlando with most of the

* Ellis' " Specimens of Early English Poetical Romances," vol. ii., p. 287 ; and Panizzi's " Essay on the Romantic Narrative Poetry of the Italians," in his edition of Boiardo and Ariosto, vol. i., p. 113.

Paladins into the pass of Roncesvalles, where the hero himself and almost all his companions are slain by the armies of Gan's fellow-traitor, Marsilius, King of Spain. They die, however, victorious; and the two royal and noble scoundrels, by a piece of prosaical justice better than poetical, are despatched like common malefactors with a halter.

There is, perhaps, no pure invention in the whole of this enlargement of old ballads and chronicles, except the characters of another giant, and of a rebel angel; for even Morgante's history, though told in a very different manner, has its prototype in the fictions of the pretended archbishop.* The Paladins are well distinguished from one another; Orlando as foremost alike in prowess and magnanimity, Rinaldo by his vehemence, Ricciardetto by his amours, Astolfo by an ostentatious rashness and self-committal; but in all these respects they appear to have been made to the author's hand. Neither does the poem exhibit any prevailing

---

* "De Vita Caroli Magni et Rolandi Historia," etc., cap. xviii., p. 39 (Ciampi's edition). The giant in Turpin is named Ferracutus, or Fergus. He was of the race of Goliath, had the strength of forty men, and was twenty cubits high. During the suspension of a mortal combat with Orlando, they discuss the mysteries of the Christian faith, which its champion explains by a variety of similes and the most beautiful beggings of the question; after which the giant stakes the credit of their respective beliefs on the event of their encounter.

force of imagery, or of expression, apart from popular idiomatic phraseology; still less, though it has plenty of infernal magic, does it present us with any magical enchantments of the alluring order, as in Ariosto ; or with love stories as good as Boiardo's, or even with any of the luxuries of landscape and description that are to be found in both of those poets ; albeit, in the fourteenth canto, there is a long *catalogue raisonné* of the whole animal creation, which a lady has worked for Rinaldo on a pavilion of silk and gold.

To these negative faults must be added the positive ones of too many trifling, unconnected, and uninteresting incidents (at least to readers who cannot taste the flavor of the racy Tuscan idiom); great occasional prolixity, even in the best as well as worst passages, not excepting Orlando's dying speeches; harshness in spite of his fluency (according to Foscolo), and even bad grammar; too many low or over-familiar forms of speech (so the graver critics allege, though, perhaps, from want of animal spirits or a more comprehensive discernment); and lastly (to say nothing of the question as to the gravity or levity of the theology), the strange exhibition of whole successive stanzas, containing as many questions or affirmations as lines, and commencing each line with the same

words.   They meet the eye like palisadoes, or a
file of soldiers, and turn truth and pathos itself
into a jest.   They were most likely imitated
from the popular ballads.   The following is the
order of words in which a young lady thinks
fit to complain of a desert, into which she has
been carried away by a giant.   After seven
initiatory O's addressed to her friends and to
life in general, she changes the key into E :

> " E' questa la mia patria dov' io nacqui ?
>   E' questo il mio palagio e 'l mio castello ?
>   E' questo il nido ov' alcun tempo giacqui ?
>   E' questo il padre e 'l mio dolce fratello ?
>   E' questo il popol dov' io tanto piacqui ?
>   E' questo il regno giusto antico e bello ?
>   E' questo il porto de la mia salute ?
>   E' questo il premio d' ogni mia virtute ?
>
> " Ove son or le mie purpuree veste ?
>   Ove son or le gemme e le ricchezze ?
>   Ove son or già le notturne feste ?
>   Ove son or le mie delicatezze ?
>   Ove son or le mie compagne oneste ?
>   Ove son or le fuggite dolcezze ?
>   Ove son or le damigelle mie ?
>   Ove son, dico ? omè, non son già quie." *
>
>   Is this the country, then, where I was born ?
>   Is this my palace, and my castle this ?
>   Is this the nest I woke in every morn ?
>   Is this my father's and my brother's kiss ?

* Canto xix., st. 21.

Is this the land they bred me to adorn?
Is this the good old bower of all my bliss?
Is this the haven of my youth and beauty?
Is this the sure reward of all my duty?

Where now are all my wardrobes and their treasures?
Where now are all my riches and my rights?
Where now are all the midnight feasts and measures?
Where now are all the delicate delights?
Where now are all the partners of my pleasures?
Where now are all the sweet of sounds and sights?
Where now are all my maidens ever near?
Where, do I say? Alas, alas, not here!

There are seven more "where nows," including lovers, and "proffered husbands," and "romances," and ending with the startling question and answer,—the counterpoint of the former close,—

" Ove son l' aspre selve e i lupi adesso
E gli orsi, e i draghi, e i tigri? Son qui presso."

Where are all the woods and forests drear,
Wolves, tigers, bears and dragons? Alas, here!

These are all very natural thoughts, and such, no doubt, as would actually pass through the mind of the young lady, in the candor of desolation; but the mechanical iteration of her mode of putting them renders them irresistibly ludicrous. It reminds us of the wager laid by the poor queen in the play of "Richard the Second," when she overhears the discourse of the gardener:

"My wretchedness *unto a row of pins*,
    They 'll talk of state."

Did Pulci expect his friend Lorenzo to keep a
grave face during the recital of these passages?
Or did he flatter himself that the comprehensive mind of his hearer could at one and the
same time be amused with the banter of some
old song and the pathos of the new one?*

* When a proper name happens to be a part of the
tautology, the look is still more extraordinary. Orlando
is remonstrating with Rinaldo on his being unseason-
ably in love :

    " Ov' è, Rinaldo, la tua gagliardia?
     Ov' è, Rinaldo, il tuo sommo potere?
     Ov' è, Rinaldo, il tuo senno di pria?
     Ov' è, Rinaldo, il tuo antivedere?
     Ov' è, Rinaldo, la tua fantasia?
     Ov' è, Rinaldo, l' arme e 'l tuo destriere?
     Ov' è, Rinaldo, la tua gloria e fama?
     Ov' è, Rinaldo, il tuo core? a la dama."

                                    Canto xvi., st. 50.

    Oh where, Rinaldo, is thy gagliardize?
    Oh where, Rinaldo, is thy might indeed?
    Oh where, Rinaldo, thy repute for wise?
    Oh where, Rinaldo, thy sagacious heed?
    Oh where, Rinaldo, thy free-thoughted eyes?
    Oh where, Rinaldo, thy good arms and steed?
    Oh where, Rinaldo, thy renown and glory?
    Oh where, Rinaldo, *thou?*—In a love-story."

The incessant repetition of the names in the burdens
of modern songs is hardly so bad as this. The single
line questions and answers in the Greek drama were
nothing to it. Yet there is a still more extraordinary
play upon words in canto xxiii., st. 49, consisting of the
description of a hermitage. It is the only one of the
kind which I remember in the poem, and would have
driven some of our old hunters after alliteration mad
with envy :—

    " La *casa cosa* parea *bretta* e *brutta*,
     Vinta dal *vento*; e la *natta* e la *notte*

The want of both good love-episodes and of
descriptions of external nature, in the "Morgante" is remarkable; for Pulci's tenderness of
heart is constantly manifest, and he describes
himself as being almost absorbed in his woods.
That he understood love well in all its force
and delicacy is apparent from a passage connected with this pavilion. The fair embroiderer,
in presenting it to her idol Rinaldo, under-
values it as a gift which his great heart nevertheless, will not disdain to accept; adding,
with the true lavishment of the passion, that

> *Stilla* le *stelle*, ch' a *tetto* era *tutto* :
> Del *pane appena* ne *dette* ta' *dotte* :
> *Pere* avea *pure*, e qualche *fratta frutta* ;
> E *svina* e *svena* di *botto* una *botte* :
> *Poscia* per *pesci lasche* prese a *l' esca* ;
> Ma il *letto allotta* a la *frasca* fu *fresca*."

> This *holy hole* was a vile *thin*-built *thing*,
> *Blown* by the *blast* ; the *night nought* else o'erhead
> But *starring stars* the *rude roof* entering ;
> Their *sup* of *supper* was no *splendid spread* ;
> *Poor pears* their fare, and such-*like libelling*
> Of Quantum suff. ;—their *butt* all *but* ;—bad bread ;—
> A *flash* of *fish* instead of *flush* of *flesh* ;
> Their bed a *frisk al-fresco, freezing fresh*.

Really, if Sir Philip Sidney and other serious and exquisite gentlemen had not sometimes taken a positively
grave interest in the like pastimes of paronomasia, one
should hardly conceive it possible to meet with them
even in tragi-comedy. Did Pulci find these also in his
ballad-authorities? If his Greek-loving critics made ob-
jections here, they had the advantage of him: unless
indeed they too, in their Alexandrian predilections, had
a sneaking regard for certain shapings of verse into
altars and hatchets, such as have been charged upon
Theocritus himself, and which might be supposed to
warrant any other conceit on occasion.

"she wishes she could give him the sun"; and that if she were to say, after all, that it was her own hands which had worked the pavilion, she should be wrong, for Love himself did it. Rinaldo wishes to thank her, but is so struck with her magnificence and affection, that the words die on his lips. The way also in which another of these loving admirers of Paladins conceives her affection for one of them, and persuades a vehemently hostile suitor quietly to withdraw his claims by presenting him with a ring and a graceful speech, is in a taste as high as any thing in Boiardo, and superior to the more animal passion of the love in their great successor.* Yet the tenderness of Pulci rather shows itself in the friendship of the Paladins for one another, and in perpetual little escapes of generous and affectionate impulse. This is one of the great charms of the "Morgante." The first adventure in the book is Orlando's encounter with three giants in behalf of a good

* See, in the original, the story of Meridiana, canto vii. King Manfredonio has come in loving hostility against her to endeavor to win her affection by his prowess. He finds her assisted by the Paladins, and engaged by her own heart to Uliviero; and in the despair of his discomfiture, expresses a wish to die by her hand. Meridiana, with graceful pity, begs his acceptance of a jewel, and recommends him to go home with his army, to which he grievingly consents. This indeed is beautiful; and perhaps I ought to have given an abstract of it, as a specimen of what Pulci could have done in this way, had he chosen.

abbot, in whom he discovers a kinsman; and this goodness and relationship combined move the Achilles of Christendom to tears. Morgante, one of these giants, who is converted, becomes a sort of squire to his conqueror, and takes such a liking to him, that, seeing him one day deliver himself not without peril out of the clutches of a devil, he longs to go and set free the whole of the other world from devils. Indeed there is no end to his affection for him. Rinaldo and other Paladins, meantime, cannot rest till they have set out in search of Orlando. They never meet or part with him without manifesting a tenderness proportionate to their valor,—the old Homeric candor of emotion. The devil Ashtaroth himself, who is a great and proud devil, assures Rinaldo, for whom he has conceived a regard, that there is good feeling (*gentilessa*) even in hell; and Rinaldo, not to hurt the feeling, answers that he has no doubt of it, or of the capability of "friendship" in that quarter; and he says he is as "sorry to part with him as with a brother." The passage will be found in our abstract. There are no such devils as these in Dante; though Milton has something like them:

> " Devil with devil damn'd
> Firm concord holds : men only disagree."

It is supposed that the character of Ashtaroth,

which is a very new and extraordinary one, and does great honor to the daring goodness of Pulci's imagination, was not lost upon Milton, who was not only acquainted with the poem, but expressly intimates the pleasure he took in it.* Rinaldo advises this devil, as Burns did Lucifer, to "take a thought and mend." Ashtaroth, who had been a seraph, takes no notice of the advice, except with a waiving of the recollection of happier times. He bids the hero farewell, and says he has only to summon him in order to receive his aid. This retention of a sense of his former angelical dignity has been noticed by Foscolo and Panizzi, the two best writers on these Italian poems.† A Cal-

---

* "Perhaps it was from that same politic drift that the devil whipt St. Jerome in a lenten dream for reading Cicero; or else it was a fantasm bred by the fever which had then seized him. For had an angel been his discipliner, unless it were for dwelling too much upon Ciceronianisms, and had chastised the reading and not the vanity, it had been plainly partial; first to correct him for grave Cicero, and not for scurrile Plautus, whom he confesses to have been reading not long before; next, to correct him only, and let so many more ancient fathers wax old in those pleasant and florid studies without the lash of such a tutoring apparition; insomuch that Basil teaches how some good use may be made of 'Margites,' a sportful poem, not now extant, writ by Homer; and why not then of 'Morgante,' an Italian romance much to the same purpose?"—"Areopagitica, a Speech for the Liberty of Unlicensed Printing," Prose Works, folio, 1697, p. 378. I quote the passage as extracted by Mr. Merivale in the preface to his "Orlando in Roncesvalles,"—Poems, vol. ii., p. 41.

† *Ut sup.*, p. 222. Foscolo's remark is to be found in his admirable article on the "Narrative and Romantic

vinist would call the expression of the sympathy
"hardened." A humanist knows it to be the
result of a spirit exquisitely softened. An unbounded tenderness is the secret of all that is
beautiful in the serious portion of our author's
genius. Orlando's good-natured giant weeps
even for the death of the scoundrel Margutte;
and the awful hero himself, at whose death nature is convulsed and the heavens open, begs
his dying horse to forgive him if ever he has
wronged it.

A charm of another sort in Pulci, and yet, in
most instances, perhaps, owing the best part of
its charmingness to its being connected with
the same feeling, is his wit. Foscolo, it is true,
says it is, in general, more severe than refined;
and it is perilous to differ with such a critic on
such a point; for much of it, unfortunately, is
lost to a foreign reader, in consequence of its
dependance on the piquant old Tuscan idiom,
and on popular sayings and allusions. Yet I
should think it impossible for Pulci in general
to be severe at the expense of some more agreeable quality; and I am sure that the portion of
his wit most obvious to a foreigner may claim,
if not to have originated, at least to have been
very like the style of one who was among its

Poems of the Italians," in the *Quarterly Review*, vol.
xxi., p. 525.

declared admirers,—and who was a very polished
writer,—Voltaire. It consists in treating an
absurdity with an air as if it were none; or as
if it had been a pure matter of course, erron-
eously mistaken for an absurdity. Thus the
good abbot, whose monastery is blockaded by
the giants (for the virtue and simplicity of his
character must be borne in mind), after observing that the ancient fathers in the desert had
not only locusts to eat, but manna, which he
has no doubt was rained down on purpose from
heaven, laments that the "relishes" provided
for himself and his brethren should have consisted of "showers of stones." The stones,
while the abbot is speaking, come thundering
down, and he exclaims: "For God's sake,
knight, come in, for the manna is falling!"
This is exactly in the style of the "Dictionnaire
Philosophique." So when Margutte is asked
what he believes in, and says he believes in
"neither black nor blue," but in a good capon,
"whether roast or boiled," the reader is forcibly
reminded of Voltaire's Traveller, *Scarmentado*,
who, when he is desired by the Tartars to declare
which of their two parties he is for, the party
of the black-mutton or the white-mutton, answers, that the dish is "equally indifferent to
him, provided it is tender." Voltaire, however,
does injustice to Pulci when he pretends that,

in matters of belief, he is like himself,—a mere
scoffer. The friend of Lucrezia Tornabuoni has
evidently the tenderest veneration for all that is
good and lovely in the Catholic faith; and whatever liberties he might have allowed himself in
professed *extravaganzas*, when an age without
Church-authority encouraged them, and a reverend canon could take part in those (it must be
acknowledged) unseemly "high jinks," he
never, in the "Morgante," when speaking in
his own person, and not in that of the worst
characters, intimates disrespect towards any
opinion which he did not hold to be irrelevant
to a right faith. It is observable that his freest
expressions are put in the mouth of the giant
Margutte, the lowest of these characters, who is
an invention of the author's, and a most extraordinary personage. He is the first unmitigated
blackguard in fiction, and is the greatest as well
as first. Pulci is conjectured, with great probability, to have designed him as a caricature of
some real person; for Margutte is a Greek who,
in point of morals, has been horribly brought
up, and some of the Greek refugees in Italy
were greatly disliked for the cynicism of their
manners and the grossness of their lives. Margutte is a glutton, a drunkard, a liar, a thief,
and a blasphemer. He boasts of having every
vice, and no virtue except fidelity; which is

meant to reconcile Morgante to his company ; but, though the latter endures and even likes it for his amusement, he gives him to understand that he looks on his fidelity as only securable by the bastinado, and makes him the subject of his practical jokes. The respectable giant Morgante dies of the bite of a crab, as if to show on what trivial chances depends the life of the strongest. Margutte laughs himself to death at sight of a monkey putting his boots on and off; as though the good-natured poet meant at once to express his contempt of a merely and grossly anti-serious mode of existence, and his consideration, nevertheless, towards the poor selfish wretch who had had no better training.

To this wit and this pathos let the reader add a style of singular ease and fluency,—rhymes often the most unexpected, but never at a loss, —a purity of Tuscan acknowledged by every body, and ranking him among the authorities of the language,—and a modesty in speaking of his own pretentions equalled only by his enthusiastic extolments of genius in others ; and the reader has before him the lively and affecting, hopeful, charitable, large-hearted Luigi Pulci, the precursor, and, in some respects, exemplar, of Ariosto, and, in Milton's opinion, a poet worth reading for the " good use " that may be made of him. It has been strangely supposed that his friend Politian, and Ficino the Platonist, not merely helped him with their books (as he takes a pride in telling us), but wrote a good deal of the latter part of the "Morgante," particularly the speculation in matters of opinion. As if (to say nothing of the difference of style) a man of genius, however lively, did not go through the gravest reflections in the course of his life, or could not enter into any theological or metaphysical question, to which he chose to direct his attention. Animal spirits themselves are too often but a counterbalance to the most thoughtful melancholy; and one fit of jaundice or hypochondria might have enabled the poet to see more visions of the unknown and the inscrutable in a single day, than perhaps ever entered the imagination of the elegant Latin scholar, or even the disciple of Plato.

HUMORS OF GIANTS.

HUMORS OF GIANTS.

TWELVE Paladins had the Emperor Charlemagne in his court; and the most wise and famous of them was Orlando. It is of him I am about to speak, and of his friend Morgante, and of Gan the traitor, who beguiled him to his death in Roncesvalles, where he sounded his horn so mightily after the dolorous rout.

It was Easter, and Charles had all his court with him in Paris, making high feast and triumph. There was Orlando, the first among them, and Ogier the Dane, and Astolfo the Englishman, and Ansuigi; and there came Angiolin of Bayonne, and Uliviero, and the gentle Berlinghieri; and there was also Avolio and Avino, and Otho of Normandy, and Richard, and the wise Namo, and the aged Salamon, and Walter of Monlione, and Baldwin who was the son of the wretched Gan. The good emperor was too happy, and oftentimes fairly groaned for joy at seeing all his Paladins together.

But Fortune stands watching in secret to baffle our designs. While Charles was thus hugging himself with delight, Orlando governed every thing at court, and this made Gan burst with envy; so that he began one day talking with Charles after the following manner: "Are we always to have Orlando for our master? I have thought of speaking to you about it a thousand times. Orlando has a great deal too much presumption. Here are we, counts, dukes, and kings, at your service, but not at his; and we have resolved not to be governed any longer by one so much younger than ourselves. You began in Aspramont to give him to understand how valiant he was, and that he did great things at that fountain; whereas, if it had not been for the good Gerard, I know very well where the victory would have been. The truth is, he has an eye upon the crown. This Charles is the worthy who has deserved so much! All your generals are afflicted at it. As for me, I shall repass those mountains over which I came to you with seventy-two counts. Do you take him for a Mars?"

Orlando happened to hear these words as he sat apart, and it displeased him with the lord of Poictiers that he should speak so, but much more that Charles should believe him. He would have killed Gan, if Uliviero had not pre-

vented him and taken his sword out of his hand ;
nay, he would have killed Charlemagne ; but
at last he went from Paris by himself, raging
with scorn and grief. He borrowed, as he went,
of Ermillina the wife of Ogier, the Dane's
sword Cortana and his horse Rondel, and proceeded on his way to Brava. His wife, Alda the
Fair, hastened to embrace him ; but while she
was saying, "Welcome, my Orlando," he was
going to strike her with his sword, for his head
was bewildered, and he took her for the traitor.
The fair Alda marvelled greatly, but Orlando
recollected himself, and she took hold of the
bridle, and he leaped from his horse, and told
her all that had passed, and rested himself with
her for some days.

He then took his leave, being still carried
away by his disdain, and resolved to pass over
into Heathendom ; and as he rode, he thought,
every step of the way, of the traitor Gan ;
and so, riding on wherever the road took
him, he reached the confines between the
Christian countries and the Pagan, and came
upon an abbey situate in a dark place in a
desert.

Now above the abbey was a great mountain,
inhabited by three fierce giants, one of whom
was named Passamonte, another Alabastro, and
the third Morgante ; and these giants used to

disturb the abbey by throwing things down upon it from the mountain with slings, so that the poor little monks could not go out to fetch wood or water. Orlando knocked, but nobody would open till the abbot was spoken to. At last the abbot came himself, and opening the door bade him welcome. The good man told him the reason of the delay, and said that since the arrival of the giants they had been so perplexed that they did not know what to do. "Our ancient fathers in the desert," quoth he, "were rewarded according to their holiness. It is not to be supposed that they lived only upon locusts; doubtless, it also rained manna upon them from heaven; but here one is regaled with stones, which the giants pour on us from the mountain. These are our nice bits and relishes. The fiercest of the three, Morgante, plucks up pines and other great trees by the roots, and casts them on us." While they were talking thus in the cemetery, there came a stone which seemed as if it would break Rondel's back.

"For God's sake, cavalier," said the abbot, "come in, for the manna is falling."

"My dear abbot," answered Orlando, "this fellow, methinks, does not wish to let my horse feed; he wants to cure him of being restive; the stone seems as if it came from a good arm."

"Yes," replied the holy father, "I did not deceive you. I think, some day or other, they will cast the mountain itself on us."

Orlando quieted his horse, and then sat down to a meal; after which he said: "Abbot, I must go and return the present that has been made to my horse." The abbot with great tenderness endeavored to dissuade him, but in vain; upon which he crossed him on the forehead, and said: "Go then; and the blessing of God be with you."

Orlando scaled the mountain, and came where Passamonte was, who, seeing him alone, measured him with his eyes, and asked him if he would stay with him for a page, promising to make him comfortable. "Stupid Saracen," said Orlando, "I come to you, according to the will of God, to be your death, and not your footboy. You have displeased his servants here, and are no longer to be endured, dog that you are!"

The giant, finding himself thus insulted, ran in a fury to his weapons; and returning to Orlando, slung at him a large stone, which struck him on the head with such force, as not only made his helmet ring again, but felled him to the earth. Passamonte thought he was dead. "What could have brought that paltry fellow here?" said he, as he turned away.

But Christ never forsakes his followers. While Passamonte was going away, Orlando recovered, and cried aloud: "How now, giant? do you fancy you have killed me? Turn back, for unless you have wings, your escape is out of the question, dog of a renegade!" The giant, greatly marvelling, turned back; and stooping to pick up a stone, Orlando, who had Cortana naked in his hand, cleft his skull; upon which, cursing Mahomet, the monster tumbled, dying and blaspheming, to the ground. Blaspheming fell the sour-hearted and cruel wretch; but Orlando, in the meanwhile, thanked the Father and the Word.

The Paladin went on, seeking for Alabastro, the second giant; who, when he saw him, endeavored to pluck up a great piece of stony earth by the roots. "Ho, ho!" cried Orlando, "you too are for throwing stones, are you?" Then Alabastro took his sling, and flung at him so large a fragment as forced Orlando to defend himself, for if it had struck him, he would no more have needed a surgeon*; but collecting his strength, he thrust his sword into the giant's breast, and the loggerhead fell dead.

* A common pleasantry in the old romances. "Galaor went in, and then the halberders attacked him on one side, and the knight on the other. He snatched an axe from one, and turned to the knight and smote him, so that he had no need of a surgeon."—Southey's "Amadis of Gaul," vol. i., p. 146.

Now Morgante, the only surviving brother, had a palace made, after giants' fashion, of earth, and boughs, and shingles, in which he shut himself up at night. Orlando knocked, and disturbed him from his sleep, so that he came staring to the door like a madman, for he had had a bewildering dream.

"Who knocks there?" quoth he.

"You will know too soon," answered Orlando; "I am come to make you do penance for your sins, like your brothers. Divine Providence has sent me to avenge the wrongs of the monks upon the whole set of you. Doubt it not; for Passamonte and Alabastro are already as cold as a couple of pilasters."

"Noble knight," said Morgante, "do me no ill; but if you are a Christian, tell me in courtesy who you are."

"I will satisfy you of my faith," replied Orlando; "I adore Christ; and if you please, you may adore him also."

"I have had a strange vision," replied Morgante, with a low voice: "I was assailed by a dreadful serpent, and called upon Mahomet in vain; then I called upon your God who was crucified, and he succored me, and I was delivered from the serpent; so I am disposed to become a Christian."

"If you keep in this mind," returned Orlando, "you shall worship the true God, and come with me and be my companion, and I will love you with perfect love. Your idols are false and vain ; the true God is the God of the Christians. Deny the unjust and villainous worship of your Mahomet, and be baptized in the name of my God, who alone is worthy."

"I am content," said Morgante.

Then Orlando embraced him, and said, "I will lead you to the abbey."

"Let us go quickly," replied Morgante, for he was impatient to make his peace with the monks.

Orlando rejoiced, saying: "My good brother, and devout withal, you must ask pardon of the abbot ; for God has enlightened you and accepted you, and he would have you practise humility."

"Yes," said Morgante, "thanks to you, your God shall henceforth be my God. Tell me your name, and afterwards dispose of me as you will." And he told him that he was Orlando.

"Blessed Jesus be thanked," said the giant, "for I have always heard you called a perfect knight ; and as I said, I will follow you all my life long."

And so conversing, they went together towards the abbey ; and by the way Orlando talked with Morgante of the dead giants, and sought

to comfort him, saying they had done the
monks a thousand injuries, and "our Scripture
says the good shall be rewarded and the evil
punished, and we must submit to the will of
God. The doctors of our Church," continued
he, "are all agreed, that if those who are glori-
fied in heaven were to feel pity for their miserable kindred who lie in such horrible confusion
in hell, their beatitude would come to nothing;
and this, you see, would plainly be unjust on the
part of God. But such is the firmness of their
faith, that what appears good to Him appears
good to them. Do what He may, they hold it
to be done well, and that it is impossible for
Him to err; so that if their very fathers and
mothers are suffering everlasting punishment,
it does not disturb them an atom. This is the
custom, I assure you, in the choirs above." *

* " Sonsi i nostri dottori accordati,
Pigliando tutti una conclusione,
Che que' che son nel ciel glorificati,
S' avessin nel pensier compassione
De' miseri parenti che dannati
Son ne lo inferno in gran confusione,
La lor felicità nulla sarebbe :
E vedi che qui ingiusto Iddio parebbe.

" Ma egli anno posto in Gesù ferma spene :
E tanto pare a lor, quanto a lui pare :
Afferman ciò ch' e' fa. che facci bene,
E che non possi in nessun modo errare :
Se padre o madre è ne l' eterne pene,
Di questo non si posson conturbare :
Che quel che piace a Dio, sol piace a loro :
Questo s' osserva ne l' eterno coro.

"A word to the wise," said Morgante; "you shall see if I grieve for my brethren, and whether or no I submit to the will of God, and behave myself like an angel. So dust to dust; and now let us enjoy ourselves. I will cut off their hands, all four of them, and take them to these holy monks, that they may be sure they are dead, and not fear to go out alone into the desert. They will then be certain also that the Lord has purified me, and taken me out of darkness, and assured to me the kingdom of heaven." So saying, the giant cut off the hands of his brethren, and left their bodies to the beasts and birds.

They went to the abbey, where the abbot was expecting Orlando in great anxiety; but the monks not knowing what had happened, ran

"Al savio suol bastar poche parole,
Disse Morgante: tu il potrai vedere,
De' miei fratelli, Orlando, se mi duole,
E s' io m' accorderò di Dio al volere,
Come tu di che in ciel servar si suole:
Morti co' morti; or pensiam di godere:
Io vo' tagliar le mani a tutti quanti,
E porterolle a que' monaci santi."

This doctrine, which is horrible blasphemy in the eyes of natural feeling, is good reasoning in Catholic and Calvinistic theology. They first make the Deity's actions a necessity from more barbarous assumption, then square them according to a dictum of the Councils, then compliment him by laying all that he has made good and kindly within us mangled and mad at his feet. Meantime they think themselves qualified to denounce Moloch and Jugghanaut.

to the abbot in great haste and alarm, saying, "Will you suffer this giant to come in ?" And when the abbot saw the giant, he changed countenance. Orlando, perceiving him thus disturbed, made haste and said : "Abbot, peace be with you ! The giant is a Christian ; he believes in Christ, and has renounced his false prophet, Mahomét." And Morgante, showing the hands in proof of his faith, the abbot thanked Heaven with great contentment of mind.

The abbot did much honor to Morgante, comparing him with St. Paul ; and they rested there many days. One day, wandering over the house, they entered a room where the abbot kept a quantity of armor ; and Morgante saw a bow which pleased him, and he fastened it on. Now there was in the place a great scarcity of water ; and Orlando said, like his good brother : "Morgante, I wish you would fetch us some water." "Command me as you please," said he ; and placing a great tub on his shoulders, he went towards a spring at which he had been accustomed to drink, at the foot of the mountain. Having reached the spring, he suddenly heard a great noise in the forest. He took an arrow from the quiver, placed it in the bow, and raising his head, saw a great herd of swine rushing towards the spring where he stood.

Morgante shot one of them clean through the head, and laid him sprawling. Another, as if in revenge, ran towards the giant, without giving him time to use a second arrow ; so he lent him a cuff on the head which broke the bone, and killed him also; which stroke the rest seeing, fled in haste through the valley. Morgante then placed the tub full of water upon one of his shoulders and the two porkers on the other, and returned to the abbey, which was at some distance, without spilling a drop.

The monks were delighted to see the fresh water, but still more the pork ; for there is no animal to whom food comes amiss. They let their breviaries therefore go to sleep awhile, and fell heartily to work, so that the cats and dogs had reason to lament the polish of the bones.

"But why do we stay here doing nothing," said Orlando one day to Morgante ; and he shook hands with the abbot, and told him he must take his leave. "I must go," said he, "and make up for lost time. I ought to have gone long ago, my good father; but I cannot tell you what I feel within me at the content I have enjoyed here in your company. I shall bear in mind and in heart with me for ever the abbot, the abbey, and this desert, so great is the love they have raised in me in so short a time. The great God, who reigns above, must thank you for me in his own abode. Bestow on us your benediction, and do not forget us in your prayers."

When the abbot heard the County Orlando talk thus, his heart melted within him for tenderness, and he said: "Knight, if we have failed in any courtesy due to your prowess and great gentleness (and indeed what we have done has been but little), pray put it to the account of our ignorance, and of the place which we inhabit. We are but poor men of the cloister, better able to regale you with masses and orisons and paternosters, than with dinners and suppers. You have so taken this heart of mine by the many noble qualities I have seen in you, that I shall be with you still wherever you go; and on the other hand, you will always be present here with me. This seems a contradiction, but you are wise and will take my meaning discreetly. You have saved the very life and spirit within us; for so much perplexity had those giants cast about our place, that the way to the Lord among us was blocked up. May He who sent you into these woods reward the justice and piety by which we are delivered from our trouble. Thanks be to Him and to you. We shall all be disconsolate at your departure. We shall grieve that we cannot detain you among us for months and years; but you do not wear these weeds; you bear arms and armor; and you may possibly merit as well in carrying those as in wearing this cap. You read your Bible, and your virtue has been the means of showing the giant the way to heaven. Go in peace, then, and prosper, whoever you may be. I do not seek your name; but if ever I am asked who it was that came among us, I shall say that it was an angel from God. If there is any armor or other thing that you would have, go into the room where it is, and take it."

"If you have any armor that would suit my companion," replied Orlando, "that I will accept with pleasure."

"Come and see," said the abbot; and they went to a room that was full of armor. Morgante looked all about, but could find nothing large enough, except a rusty breast-plate, which fitted him marvellously. It had belonged to an enormous giant, who was killed there of old by Orlando's father, Milo of Angrante. There was a painting on the wall which told the whole story: how the giant had laid cruel and long siege to the abbey; and how he had been overthrown at last by the great Milo. Orlando seeing this, said within himself: "O God, unto whom all things are known, how came Milo here, who destroyed this giant?" And reading certain inscriptions which were there, he could no longer keep a firm countenance, but the tears ran down his cheeks.

When the abbot saw Orlando weep, and his brow redden, and the light of his eyes become child-like for sweetness, he asked him the reason; but, finding him still dumb with emotion, he said, "I do not know whether you are overpowered by admiration of what is painted in this chamber. You must know that I am of high descent, though not through lawful wedlock. I believe I may say I am nephew or sister's son to no less a man than that Rinaldo, who was so great a Paladin in the world, though my own father was not of lawful mother. Ansuigi was his name; my own, out in the world, was Chiaramonte; and this Milo was my father's brother. Ah, gentle baron, for blessed Jesus' sake, tell me what name is yours!"

Orlando, all glowing with affection, and bathed in tears, replied, "My dear abbot and cousin, he before you is your Orlando." Upon this, they ran for tenderness into each other's arms, weeping on both sides with a sovereign affection, too high to be expressed. The abbot was so overjoyed, that he seemed as if he would never have done embracing Orlando. "By what fortune," said the knight, "do I find you in this obscure place? Tell me, my dear abbot, how was it you became a monk, and did not follow arms, like myself and the rest of us?"

"It is the will of God," replied the abbot, hastening to give his feelings utterance. "Many and divers are the paths he points out for us by which to arrive at his city; some walk it with the sword—some with pastoral staff. Nature makes the inclination different, and therefore there are different ways for us to take: enough if we all arrive safely at one and the same place, the last as well as the first. We are all pilgrims through many kingdoms. We all wish to go to Rome, Orlando; but we go picking out our journey through different roads. Such is the trouble in body and soul brought upon us by that sin of the old apple. Day and night am I here with my book in hand—day and night do you ride about, holding your sword, and sweating oft both in sun and shadow; and all to get round at last to the home from which we departed—I say, all out of anxiety and hope to get back to our home of old." And the giant hearing them talk of these things, shed tears also.

The Paladin and the giant quitted the abbey, the one on horseback and the other on foot, and journeyed through the desert till they came to a magnificent castle, the door of which stood open. They entered, and found rooms furnished in the most splendid manner—beds covered with cloth of gold, and floors rejoicing in variegated marbles. There was even a feast prepared in the saloon, but nobody to eat it, or to speak to them.

Orlando suspected some trap, and did not quite like it; but Morgante thought nothing worth considering but the feast. "Who cares for the host," said he, "when there 's such a dinner? Let us eat as much as we can, and bear off the rest. I always do that when I have the picking of castles."

They accordingly sat down, and being very hungry with their day's journey, devoured heaps of the good things before them, eating with all the vigor of health, and drinking to a pitch of weakness.* They sat late in this manner enjoying themselves, and then retired for the night into rich beds.

But what was their astonishment in the morning at finding that they could not get out of the place! There was no door. All the entrances had vanished, even to any feasible window.

"We must be dreaming," said Orlando.

"My dinner was no dream, I 'll swear," said

---

* " E furno al bere infermi, al mangiar sani."

I am not sure that I am right in my construction of this passage. Perhaps Pulci means to say, that they had the appetites of men in health, and the thirst of a fever.

the giant. "As for the rest, let it be a dream if it pleases."

Continuing to search up and down, they at length found a vault with a tomb in it; and out of the tomb came a voice, saying: "You must encounter with me, or stay here for ever. Lift, therefore, the stone that covers me."

"Do you hear that?" said Morgante; "I'll have him out, if it's the devil himself. Perhaps it's two devils, Filthy-dog and Foul-mouth, or Itching and Evil-tail." *

"Have him out," said Orlando, "whoever he is, even were it as many devils as were rained out of heaven into the centre."

Morgante lifted up the stone, and out leaped, surely enough, a devil in the likeness of a dried-up dead body, black as a coal. Orlando seized him, and the devil grappled with Orlando. Morgante was for joining him, but the Paladin bade him keep back. It was a hard struggle, and the devil grinned and laughed, till the giant, who was a master of wrestling, could bear it no longer: so he doubled him up, and, in spite of all his efforts, thrust him back into the tomb.

"You'll never get out," said the devil, "if you leave me shut up."

*Caygnazzo, Farfarello, Libicocco, and Malacoda; names of devils in Dante.

"Why not?" inquired the Paladin.

"Because your giant's baptism and my deliverance must go together," answered the devil. "If he is not baptized, you can have no deliverance; and if I am not delivered, I can prevent it still, take my word for it."

Orlando baptized the giant. The two companions then issued forth, and hearing a mighty noise in the house, looked back, and saw it all vanished.

"I could find it in my heart," said Morgante, "to go down to those same regions below, and make all the devils disappear in like manner. Why shouldn't we do it? We'd set free all the poor souls there. Egad, I'd cut off Minos' tail —I'd pull out Charon's beard by the roots— make a sop of Phlegyas, and a sup of Phlegethon—unseat Pluto—kill Cerberus and the Furies with a punch of the face a-piece—and set Beelzebub scampering like a dromedary."

"You might find more trouble than you wot of," quoth Orlando, "and get worsted besides. Better keep the straight path, than thrust your head into out-of-the-way places."

Morgante took his lord's advice, and went straightforward with him through many great adventures, helping him with loving good-will as often as he was permitted, sometimes as his pioneer, and sometimes as his finisher of troublesome work, such as a slaughter of some thousands of infidels. Now he chucked a spy into a river—now felled a rude ambassador to the earth (for he did n't stand upon ceremony) —now cleared a space round him in battle with the clapper of an old bell which he had found at the monastery—now doubled up a king in his tent, and bore him away, tent and all, and a Paladin with him, because he would not let the Paladin go.

In the course of these services, the giant was left to take care of a lady, and lost his master for a time; but the office being at an end, he set out to rejoin him, and, arriving at a cross-road, met with a very extraordinary personage.

This was a giant huger than himself, swarthy-faced, horrible, brutish. He came out of a wood, and appeared to be journeying somewhere. Morgante, who had the great bell-clapper above-mentioned in his hand, struck it on the ground with astonishment, as much as to say, "Who the devil is this?" and then set himself on a stone by the way-side to observe the creature.

"What 's your name traveller?" said Morgante, as it came up.

"My name 's Margutte," said the phenomenon. "I intended to be a giant myself, but altered my mind, you see, and stopped half-way; so that I am only twenty feet or so."

"I'm glad to see you," quoth his brother-
giant. "But tell me, are you Christian or
Saracen? Do you believe in Christ or in
Apollo?"

"To tell you the truth," said the other, "I
believe neither in black nor blue, but in a good
capon, whether it be roast or boiled. I believe
sometimes also in butter, and, when I can get
it, in new wine, particularly the rough sort; but,
above all, I believe in wine that's good and
old. Mahomet's prohibition of it is all moon-
shine. I am the son, you must know, of a Greek
nun and a Turkish bishop; and the first thing
I learned was to play the fiddle. I used to sing
Homer to it. I was then concerned in a brawl
in a mosque, in which the old bishop somehow
happened to be killed; so I tied a sword to my
side, and went to seek my fortune, accompanied
by all the possible sins of Turk and Greek.
People talk of the seven deadly sins; but I have
seventy-seven that never quit me, summer or
winter; by which you may judge of the amount
of my venial ones. I am a gambler, a cheat, a
ruffian, a highwayman, a pickpocket, a glutton
(at beef or blows); have no shame whatever;
love to let everybody know what I can do; lie,
besides, about what I can't do; have a particular
attachment to sacrilege; swallow perjuries like
figs; never give a farthing to anybody, but beg

of everybody, and abuse them into the bargain ;
look upon not spilling a drop of liquor as the
chief of all the cardinal virtues ; but must own
I am not much given to assassination, murder
being inconvenient ; and one thing I am bound
to acknowledge, which is, that I never betrayed
a messmate.''

''That 's as well,'' observed Morgante ; ''because you see, as you don't believe in any thing
else, I 'd have you believe in this bell-clapper of
mine. So now, as you have been candid with
me, and I am well instructed in your ways,
we 'll pursue our journey together.''

The best of giants in those days, were not
scrupulous in their modes of living ; so that one
of the best and one of the worst got on pretty
well together, emptying the larders on the road,
and paying nothing but douses on the chops.
When they could find no inn, they hunted ele-
phants and crocodiles. Morgante, who was the
braver of the two, delighted to banter, and
sometimes to cheat, Margutte ; and he ate up all
the fare ; which made the other, notwithstanding the credit he gave himself for readiness of
wit and tongue, cut a very sorry figure, and seriously remonstrate : ''I reverence you,'' said
Margutte, ''in other matters ; but in eating, you
really don't behave well. He who deprives me
of my share at meals is no friend ; at every

mouthful of which he robs me, I seem to lose
an eye. I 'm for sharing every thing to a nice-
ty, even if it be no better than a fig."

"You are a fine fellow," said Morgante;
"you gain upon me very much. You are 'the
master of those who know.'"*

So saying, he made him put some wood on
the fire, and perform a hundred other offices to
render every thing snug; and then he slept: and
next day he cheated his great scoundrelly companion at drink, as he had done the day before
at meat; and the poor shabby devil complained; and Morgante laughed till he was
ready to burst, and again and again always
cheated him.

There was a levity, nevertheless, in Margutte, which restored his spirits on the slight-
est glimpse of good-fortune; and if he realized a
hearty meal, he became the happiest, beastli-
est, and most confident of giants. The companions, in the course of their journey, delivered a damsel from the clutches of three other
giants. She was the daughter of a great lord;
and when she got home, she did honor to Morgante as to an equal, and put Margutte into the
kitchen, where he was in a state of bliss. He
did nothing but swill, stuff, surfeit, be sick,

* "Il maestro di color che sanno." A jocose application of Dante's praise of Aristotle.

play at dice, cheat, filch, go to sleep, guzzle again, laugh, chatter, and tell a thousand lies.

Morgante took leave of the young lady, who made him rich presents. Margutte, seeing this, and being always drunk and impudent, daubed his face like a Christmas clown, and making up to her with a frying-pan in his hand, demanded "something for the cook." The fair hostess gave him a jewel: and the vagabond showed such a brutal eagerness in seizing it with his filthy hands, and making not the least acknowledgment, that when they got out of the house, Morgante was ready to fell him to the earth. He called him scoundrel and poltroon, and said he had disgraced him forever.

"Softly!" said the brute-beast. "Didn't you take me with you, knowing what sort of fellow I was? Didn't I tell you I had every sin and shame under heaven; and have I deceived you by the exhibition of a single virtue?"

Morgante could not help laughing at a candor of this excessive nature. So they went on their way till they came to a wood, where they rested themselves by a fountain, and Margutte fell fast asleep. He had a pair of boots on, which Morgante felt tempted to draw off, that he might see what he would do on waking. He accordingly did so, and threw them to a little distance among the bushes. The sleeper awoke in good time, and, looking and searching round about, suddenly burst into roars of laughter. A monkey had got the boots, and sat pulling them on and off, making the most ridiculous gestures. The monkey busied himself, and the light-minded drunkard laughed; and at every fresh gesticulation of the new boot-wearer, the laugh grew louder and more tremendous, till at length it was found impossible to be restrained. The glutton had a laughing fit. In vain he tried to stop himself; in vain his fingers would have loosened the buttons of his doublet, to give his lungs room to play. They could n't do it ; so he laughed and roared till he burst. The snap was like the splitting of a cannon. Morgante ran up to him, but it was of no use. He was dead.

Alas! it was not the only death ; it was not even the most trivial cause of a death. Giants are big fellows, but Death 's a bigger, though he may come in a little shape. Morgante had succeeded in joining his master. He helped him to take Babylon ; he killed a whale for him at sea that obstructed his passage ; he played the part of a main-sail during a storm, holding out his arms and a great hide ; but on coming to shore, a crab bit him in the heel ; and behold the lot of the great giant—he died! He laughed, and thought it a very little thing, but it proved a mighty one. "He made the East tremble," said Orlando; "and the bite of a crab has slain him!"

O life of ours, weak, and a fallacy!*

Orlando embalmed his huge friend, and had him taken to Babylon, and honorably interred; and after many an adventure, in which he regretted him, his own days were closed by a far baser, though not so petty a cause.

How shall I speak of it? exclaims the poet. How think of the horrible slaughter about to fall on the Christians and their greatest men, so that not a dry eye shall be left in France? How express my disgust at the traitor Gan, whose heart a thousand pardons from his sovereign, and the most undeserved rescues of him by the warrior he betrayed, could not shame or soften? How mourn the weakness of Charles, always deceived by him, and always trusting? How dare to present to my mind the good, the great, the ever-generous Orlando, brought by the traitor into the doleful pass of Roncesvalles and the hands of myriads of his enemies, so that even his superhuman strength availed not to deliver him out of the slaughter-house, and he blew the blast with his dying breath, which was the mightiest, the farthest heard, and the most

* " O vita nostra, debole e fallace!"

melancholy sound that ever came to the ears of the undeceived?

Gan was known well to every body but his confiding sovereign. The Paladins knew him well; and in their moments of indignant disgust often told him so, though they spared him the consequences of his misdeeds, and even incurred the most frightful perils to deliver him out of the hands of his enemies. But he was brave; he was in favor with the sovereign, who was also their kinsman; and they were loyal and loving men, and knew that the wretch envied them for the greatness of their achievements, and might do the state a mischief; so they allowed themselves to take a kind of scornful pleasure in putting up with him. Their cousin Malagigi, the enchanter, had himself assisted Gan, though he knew him best of all, and had prophesied that the innumerable endeavors of his envy to destroy his king and country would bring some terrible evil at last to all Christendom. The evil, alas! is at hand. The doleful time has come. It will be followed, it is true, by a worse fate of the wretch himself; but not till the valleys of the Pyrenees have run rivers of blood, and all France is in mourning.

NOTICE.

THIS is the

> " sad and fearful story
> Of the Roncesvalles fight " ;

an event which national and religious exaggeration impressed deeply on the popular mind of Europe. Hence Italian romances and Spanish ballads ; hence the famous passage in Milton :

> ' When Charlemain with all his peerage fell
> By Fontarabbia " :

hence Dante's record of the *dolorosa rotta* (dolorous rout) in the " Inferno," where he compares the voice of Nimrod with the horn sounded by the dying Orlando ; hence the peasant in Cervantes, who is met by Don Quixote singing the battle as he comes along the road in the morning ; and hence the song of Roland actually thundered forth by the army of William the Conqueror as they advanced against the English.

But Charlemagne did not " fall," as Milton has stated. Nor does Pulci make him do so. In this respect, if in little else, the Italian poet adhered to the fact. The whole story is a remarkable instance of what can be done by poetry and popularity towards misrepresenting and aggrandizing a petty though striking adventure. The simple fact was the cutting off the rear of Charlemagne's army by the revolted Gascons, as he returned from a successful expedition into Spain. Two or three only of his nobles perished, among whom was his nephew Roland, the obscure warden of his marches of Brittany. But Charlemagne was the temporal head of Christendom ; the poets constituted his nephew its champion ; and hence all the glories and superhuman exploits of the Orlando of Pulci and Ariosto. The whole assumption of the wickedness of the Saracens, particularly of the then Saracen king of Spain, whom Pulci's authority, the pseudo-archbishop, Turpin, strangely called Marsilius, was nothing but a pious fraud : the pretended Marsilius having been no less a person than the great and good Abdoùlrahmaùn the First, who wrested the dominion of that country out of the hands of the usurpers of his family rights. Yet so potent and longlived are the most extravagant fictions, when genius has put its heart into them, that to this day we read of the devoted Orlando and his friends not only with gravity, but with the liveliest emotion.

THE BATTLE OF RONCESVALLES.

THE BATTLE OF RONCESVALLES.

A MISERABLE man am I, cries the poet;
for Orlando, beyond a doubt, died in Roncesvalles; and die, therefore, he must in my
verses. Altogether impossible is it to save
him. I thought to make a pleasant ending of
this my poem, so that it should be happier
somehow, throughout, than melancholy; but
though Gan will die at last, Orlando must die
before him, and that makes a tragedy of all. I
had a doubt, whether, consistently with the
truth, I could give the reader even that sorry
satisfaction; for at the beginning of the dreadful battle, Orlando's cousin, Rinaldo, who was
said to have joined it before it was over, and
there, as well as afterwards, to have avenged
his death, was far away from the seat of slaughter, in Egypt; and how was I to suppose that
he could arrive soon enough in the valleys of
the Pyrenees? But an angel upon earth showed
me the secret, even Angelo Poliziano, the glory
of his age and country. He informed me how
Arnauld, the Provençal poet, had written of

this very matter, and brought the Paladin from
Egypt to France by means of the wonderful
skill in occult science possessed by his cousin
Malagigi—a wonder to the ignorant, but not so
marvellous to those who know that all the creation is full of wonders, and who have different
modes of relating the same events. By and by
a great many things will be done in the world,
of which we have no conception now, and people will be inclined to believe them works of
the devil, when, in fact, they will be very good
works, and contribute to angelical effects,
whether the devil be forced to have a hand in
them or not; for evil itself can work only in
subordination to good. So listen when the
astonishment comes, and reflect and think the
best. Meantime, we must speak of another
and more truly devilish astonishment, and of
the pangs of mortal flesh and blood.

The traitor Gan, for the fiftieth time, had
secretly brought the infidels from all quarters
against his friend and master, the Emperor
Charles; and Charles, by the help of Orlando,
had conquered them all. The worst of them,
Marsilius, king of Spain, had agreed to pay the
court of France tribute; and Gan, in spite of
all the suspicions he excited in this particular
instance, and his known villainy at all times,
had succeeded in persuading his credulous sov-

ereign to let him go ambassador into Spain,
where he put a final seal to his enormities, by
plotting the destruction of his employer, and
the special overthrow of Orlando. Charles was
now old and white-haired, and Gan was so too ;
but the one was only confirmed in his credulity,
and the other in his crimes. The traitor embraced Orlando over and over again at taking
leave, praying him to write if he had any thing
to say before the arrangements with Marsilius,
and taking such pains to seem loving and sincere, that his villany was manifest to every one
but the old monarch. He fastened with equal
tenderness on Uliviero, who smiled contemptuously in his face, and thought to himself, "You
may make as many fair speeches as you choose,
but you lie." All the other Paladins who were
present thought the same, and they said as
much to the emperor; adding, that on no account should Gan be sent ambassador to Marsilius. But Charles was infatuated. His beard
and his credulity had grown old together.

Gan was received with great honor in Spain
by Marsilius. The king, attended by his lords,
came fifteen miles out of Saragossa to meet him,
and then conducted him into the city amid
tumults of delight. There was nothing for several days but balls, and games, and exhibitions
of chivalry, the ladies throwing flowers on the

heads of the French knights, and the people shouting, "France! France! Mountjoy and St. Denis!"

Gan made a speech, "like a Demosthenes," to King Marsilius in public; but he made him another in private, like nobody but himself. The king and he were sitting in a garden; they were traitors both, and began to understand, from one another's looks, that the real object of the ambassador was yet to be discussed. Marsilius accordingly assumed a more than usually cheerful and confidential aspect; and, taking his visitor by the hand, said: "You know the proverb, Mr. Ambassador—'At dawn, the mountain; afternoon, the fountain.' Different things at different hours. So here is a fountain to accommodate us."

It was a very beautiful fountain, so clear that you saw your face in it as in a mirror; and the spot was encircled with fruit-trees that quivered with the fresh air. Gan praised it very much, contriving to insinuate, on one subject, his satisfaction with the glimpses he got into another. Marsilius understood him; and as he resumed the conversation, and gradually encouraged a mutual disclosure of their thoughts, Gan, without appearing to look him in the face, was enabled to do so by contemplating the royal visage in the water, where he saw its expression

become more and more what he desired. Marsilius, meantime, saw the like symptoms in the
face of Gan. By degrees, he began to touch on
that dissatisfaction with Charlemagne and his
court, which he knew was in both their minds :
he lamented, not as to the ambassador, but as
to the friend, the injuries which he said he had
received from Charles in the repeated attacks
on his dominions, and the emperor's wish to
crown Orlando king of them ; till at length he
plainly uttered his belief, that if that tremendous Paladin were but dead, good men would
get their rights, and his visitor and himself have
all things at their disposal.

Gan heaved a sigh, as if he was unwillingly
compelled to allow the force of what the king
said ; but, unable to contain himself long, he
lifted up his face, radiant with triumphant wickedness, and exclaimed : '' Every word you utter
is truth. Die he must ; and die also must Uliviero, who struck me that foul blow at court.
Is it treachery to punish affronts like those? I
have planned every thing ; I have settled every
thing already with their besotted master. Orlando could not be expected to be brought
hither, where he has been accustomed to look
for a crown ; but he will come to the Spanish
borders—to Roncesvalles—for the purpose of
receiving the tribute. Charles will await him,

at no great distance, in St. John Pied de Port. Orlando will bring but a small band with him; you, when you meet him, will have secretly your whole army at your back. You surround him; and who receives tribute then?"

The new Judas had scarcely uttered these words, when the delight of him and his associate was interrupted by a change in the face of nature. The sky was suddenly overcast; it thundered and lightened; a laurel was split in two from head to foot; the fountain ran into burning blood; there was an earthquake, and the carob-tree under which Gan was sitting, and which was of the species on which Judas Iscariot hung himself, dropped some of its fruit on his head. The hair of the head rose in horror.

Marsilius, as well as Gan, was appalled at this omen; but on assembling his soothsayers, they came to the conclusion that the laurel-tree turned the omen against the emperor, the successor of the Cæsars; though one of them renewed the consternation of Gan, by saying that he did not understand the meaning of the tree of Judas, and intimating that perhaps the ambassador could explain it. Gan relieved his consternation with anger; the habit of wickedness prevailed over all considerations; and the king prepared to march for Roncesvalles at the head of all his forces.

Gan wrote to Charlemagne, to say how humbly
and properly Marsilius was coming to pay the
tribute into the hands of Orlando, and how
handsome it would be of the emperor to meet
him half way, as agreed upon, at St. John Pied
de Port, and so be ready to receive him, after
the payment, at his footstool. He added a brilliant account of the tribute and its accompany-
ing presents. They included a crown in the
shape of a garland which had a carbuncle in it
that gave light in darkness; two lions of an
"immeasurable length, and aspects that frightened every body"; some "lively buffaloes,"
leopards, crocodiles, and giraffes; arms and
armor of all sorts; and apes and monkeys seated
among the rich merchandise that loaded the
backs of the camels. This imaginary treasure
contained, furthermore, two enchanted spirits,
called "Floro and Faresse," who were confined
in a mirror, and were to tell the emperor wonderful things, particularly Floro (for there is
nothing so nice in its details as lying); and Orlando was to have heaps of caravans full of
Eastern wealth, and a hundred white horses, all
with saddles and bridles of gold. There was a
beautiful vest, too, for Uliviero, all over jewels,
worth ten thousand "seraffi," or more.

The good emperor wrote in turn to say how
pleased he was with the ambassador's diligence,

and that matters were arranged precisely as he wished. His court, however, had its suspicions still. Nobody could believe that Gan had not some new mischief in contemplation. Little, nevertheless, did they imagine, after the base endeavors he had but lately made against them, that he had immediately plotted a new and greater one, and that his object in bringing Charles into the neighborhood of Roncesvalles was to deliver him more speedily into the hands of Marsilius, in the event of the latter's destruction of Orlando.

Orlando, however, did as his lord and sovereign desired. He went to Roncesvalles, accompanied by a moderate train of warriors, not dreaming of the atrocity that awaited him. Gan himself, meantime, had hastened on to France before Marsilius, in order to show himself free and easy in the presence of Charles, and secure the success of his plot; while Marsilius, to make assurance doubly sure, brought into the passes of Roncesvalles no less than three armies, who were successively to fall on the Paladin, in case of the worst, and so extinguish him with numbers. He had also, by Gan's advice, brought heaps of wine and good cheer to be set before his victims in the first instance; "for that," said the traitor, "will render the onset the more effective, the feasters being unarmed; and, sup-

posing prodigies of valor to await even the attack of your second army, you will have no
trouble with your third. One thing, however,
I must not forget," added he; "my son Baldwin is sure to be with Orlando; you must take
care of his life for my sake."

"I give him this vest off my own body," said
the king; "let him wear it in the battle, and
have no fear. My soldiers shall be directed not
to touch him."

Gan went away rejoicing to France. He embraced the court and his sovereign all round,
with the air of a man who had brought them
nothing but blessings; and the old king wept
for very tenderness and delight.

"Something is going on wrong, and looks
very black," thought Malagigi, the good wizard; "and Rinaldo is not here, and it is indis-
pensably necessary that he should be. I must
find out where he is, and Ricciardetto too, and
send for them with all speed, and at any price."

Malagigi called up, by his art, a wise, terrible,
and cruel spirit, named Ashtaroth; no light
personage to deal with—no little spirit, such as
plays tricks with you like a fairy. A much
blacker visitant was this.

"Tell me, and tell me truly of Rinaldo," said
Malagigi to the spirit.

Hard looked the demon at the Paladin, and

said nothing. His aspect was clouded and violent. He wished to see whether his summoner retained all the force of his art.

The enchanter, with an aspect still cloudier, bade Ashtaroth lay down that look. While giving this order, he also made signs indicative of a disposition to resort to angrier compulsion; and the devil, apprehending that he would confine him in some hateful place, loosened his tongue, and said: "You have not told me what you desire to know of Rinaldo."

"I desire to know what he has been doing, and where he is," returned the enchanter.

"He has been conquering and baptizing the world, east and west," said the demon, "and is now in Egypt with Ricciardetto."

"And what has Gan been plotting with Marsilius," inquired Malagigi, "and what is to come of it?"

"On neither of those points can I enlighten you," said the devil. "I was not attending to Gan at the time, and we fallen spirits know not the future. Had we done so, we had not been so willing to incur the danger of falling. All I discern is, that by the signs and comets in the heavens, something dreadful is about to happen —something very strange, treacherous, and bloody; and that Gan has a seat ready prepared for him in hell."

"Within three days," cried the enchanter, loudly," "fetch Rinaldo and Ricciardetto into the pass of Roncesvalles. Do it, and I hereby undertake never to summon thee more."

"Suppose they will not trust themselves with me," said the spirit.

"Enter Rinaldo's horse, and bring him, whether he trust thee or not."

"It shall be done," returned the demon; "and my serving-devil Foul-Mouth, or Fire-Red, shall enter the horse of Ricciardetto. Doubt it not. Am I not wise, and thyself powerful?"

There was an earthquake, and Ashtaroth disappeared.

Marsilius has now made his first movement towards the destruction of Orlando, by sending before him his vassal-king Blanchardin with his presents of wines and other luxuries. The temperate but courteous hero took them in good part, and distributed them as the traitor wished; and then Blanchardin, on pretence of going forward to salute Charlemagne at St. John Pied de Port, returned and put himself at the head of the second army, which was the post assigned him by his liege lord. The device on his flag was an "Apollo" on a field azure. King Falseron, whose son Orlando had slain in battle, headed the first army, the device of which was a black figure of the devil Belphegor on a dapple-gray field. The third army was under King Balugante, and had for ensign a Mahomet with golden wings in a field of red. Marsilius made a speech to them at night, in which he confessed his ill faith, but defended it on the ground of Charles' hatred of their religion, and of the example of "Judith and Holofernes." He said that he had not come there to pay tribute and sell his countrymen for slaves, but to make all Christendom pay tribute to them as conquerors; and he concluded by recommending to their good-will the son of his friend Gan, whom they would know by the vest he had sent him, and who was the only soul among the Christians they were to spare.

This son of Gan, meantime, and several of the Paladins who were disgusted with Charles' credulity, and anxious at all events to be with Orlando, had joined the hero in the fated valley; so that the little Christian host, considering the tremendous valor of their lord and his friends, and the comparative inefficiency of that of the infidels, were at any rate not to be sold for nothing. Rinaldo, alas! the second thunderbolt of Christendom, was destined not to be there in time to save their lives. He could only avenge the dreadful tragedy, and prevent still worse consequences to the whole Christian court and empire. The Paladins had in vain begged Orlando to be on his guard against treachery, and send for a more numerous body of men. The great heart of the Champion of the Faith was unwilling to think the worst as long as he could help it. He refused to summon aid that might be superfluous; neither would he do any thing but what his liege lord had desired. And yet he could not wholly repress a misgiving. A shadow had fallen on his heart, great and cheerful as it was. The anticipations of his friends disturbed him, in spite of the face with which he met them. I am not sure that he did not, by a certain instinctive foresight, expect death itself; but he felt bound not to encourage the impression. Besides, time pressed; the moment of the looked-for tribute was at hand; and little combinations of circumstances determine often the greatest events.

King Blanchardin had brought Orlando's people a luxurious supper; King Marsilius was to arrive early next day with the tribute; and Uliviero accordingly, with the morning sun, rode forth to reconnoitre and see if he could discover the peaceful pomp of the Spanish court in the distance. Guottibuoffi was with him, a warrior who had expected the very worst, and repeatedly implored Orlando to believe it possible. Uliviero and he rode up the mountain nearest them, and from the top of it beheld the first army of Marsilius already forming in the passes.

"O Guottibuoffi!" exclaimed he, "behold thy prophecies come true! behold the last day of the glory of Charles! Everywhere I see the arms of the traitors around us. I feel Paris tremble all the way through France, to the ground beneath my feet. O Malagigi, too much in the right wert thou! O devil Gan, this, then, is the consummation of thy good offices!"

Uliviero put spurs to his horse and galloped back down the mountain to Orlando.

"Well," cried the hero, "what news?"

"Bad news," said his cousin; "such as you would not hear of yesterday. Marsilius is here in arms, and all the world has come with him."

The Paladins pressed round Orlando, and entreated him to sound his horn, in token that he needed help. His only answer was to mount his horse, and ride up the mountain with Sansonetto.

As soon, however, as he cast forth his eyes and beheld what was round about him, he turned in sorrow, and looked down into Roncesvalles, and said: "O valley, miserable indeed! the blood that is shed in thee this day will color thy name forever."

Many of the Paladins had ridden after him, and they again pressed him to sound his horn, if only in pity to his own people. He said : "If Cæsar and Alexander were here, Scipio, and Hannibal, and Nebuchadnezzar with all his flags, and Death stared me in the face with his knife in his hand, never would I sound my horn for the baseness of fear."

Orlando's little camp were furious against the Saracens. They armed themselves with the greatest impatience. There was nothing but lacing of helmets and mounting of horses ; and good Archbishop Turpin went from rank to rank, exhorting and encouraging the warriors of Christ. Accoutrements and habiliments were put on the wrong way ; words and deeds mixed in confusion ; men running against one another out of very absorption in themselves ; all the place full of cries of "Arm ! arm ! the enemy !" and the trumpets clanged over all against the mountain echoes.

Orlando and his captains withdrew for a moment to consultation. He fairly groaned for sorrow, and at first had not a word to say ; so wretched he felt at having brought his people to die in Roncesvalles.

Uliviero spoke first. He could not resist the opportunity of comforting himself a little in his despair with referring to his unheeded advice.

"You see, cousin," said he, "what has come at last. Would to God you had attended to what I said; to what Malagigi said; to what we all said! I told you Marsilius was nothing but an anointed scoundrel. Yet forsooth he was to bring us tribute! and Charles is this moment expecting his mummeries at St. John Pied de Port! Did ever any body believe a word that Gan said, but Charles? And now you see this rotten fruit has come to a head; this medlar has got its crown."

Orlando said nothing in answer to Uliviero; for in truth he had nothing to say. He broke away to give orders to the camp; bade them take refreshment; and then addressing both officers and men, he said: "I confess that if it had entered my heart to conceive the king of Spain to be such a villain, never would you have seen this day. He has exchanged with me a thousand courtesies and good words; and I thought that the worse enemies we had been before, the better friends we had become now. I fancied every human being capable of this kind of virtue on a good opportunity, saving, indeed, such base-hearted wretches as can never forgive their very forgivers; and of these I certainly did not suppose him to be one. Let us die, if we must die, like honest and gallant men; so that it shall be said of us, it was only our bodies that died. It becomes our souls to be invincible, and our glory immortal. Our motto must be, 'A good heart and no hope.' The reason why I did not sound the horn was, partly because I thought it did not become us, and partly because our liege lord could be of little use, even if he heard it. Let Gan have his glut of us, like a carrion crow; but let him find us under heaps of his Saracens—an example for all time. Heaven, my friends, is with us, if earth is against us. Methinks I see it open this moment, ready to receive our souls amidst crowns of glory; and therefore, as the champion of God's church, I give you my benediction; and the good archbishop here will absolve you; and so, please God, we shall all go to heaven and be happy."

And with these words Orlando sprang to his horse, crying, "Away against the Saracens!" but he had no sooner turned his face than he wept bitterly, and said, "O holy Virgin, think not of me, the sinner Orlando, but have pity on these thy servants."

Archbishop Turpin did as Orlando said, giving the whole band his benediction at once, and absolving them from their sins, so that every body took comfort in the thought of dying for Christ; and thus they embraced one another, weeping; and then lance was put to thigh, and the banner was raised that was won in the jousting at Aspramont.

And now with a mighty dust and an infinite sound of horns and tambours and trumpets, which came filling the valley, the first army of the infidels made its appearance, horses neighing, and a thousand pennants flying in the air. King Falseron led them on, saying to his officers: " Now, gentlemen, recollect what I said ; the first battle is for the leaders only ; and above all, let nobody dare to lay a finger on Orlando. He belongs to myself. The revenge of my son's death is mine. I will cut the man down that comes between us."

" Now, friends," said Orlando, "every man for himself, and St. Michael for us all. There is no one here that is not a perfect knight."

And he might well say it ; for the flower of all France was there, except Rinaldo and Ricciardetto ; every man a picked man ; all friends and constant companions of Orlando. There was Richard of Normandy, Guottibuoffi, and Uliviero, and Count Anselm, and Avolio, and Avino, and the gentle Berlinghieri, and his brother, and Sansonetto, and the good Duke Egibard, and Astolfo the Englishman, and Angiolin of Bayona, and all the other Paladins of France, excepting those two whom I have mentioned. And so the captains of the little troop

and of the great array sat looking at one another, and singling one another out, as the latter
came on ; and then either side began raising
their war-cries, and the mob of the infidels
halted, and the knights put spear in rest, and
ran for a while, two and two in succession, each
one against the other.

Astolfo was the first to move. He ran against
Arlotto of Soria ; and Angiolin then ran against
Malducco ; and Mazzarigi the Renegade came
against Avino ; and Uliviero was borne forth by
his horse Rondel, who could n't stand still,
against Malprimo, the first of the captains of
Falseron.

And now lances began to be painted red,
without any brush but themselves ; and the
new color extended itself to the bucklers, and
the cuishes, and the cuirasses, and trappings
of the steeds.

Astolfo thrusts his antagonist's body out of
the saddle, and his soul into the other world ;
and Angiolin gave and took a terrible blow with
Malducco ; but his horse bore him onward ; and
Avino had something of the like encounter with
Mazzarigi ; but Uliviero, though he received
a thrust which hurt him, sent his lance right
through the heart of Malprimo.

Falseron was daunted at this blow. "Verily,"
thought he, "this is a miracle." Uliviero did

not press on among the Saracens, his wound
was too painful ; but Orlando now put himself
and his whole band into motion, and you may
guess what an uproar ensued. The sound of
the rattling of the blows and helmets was as if
the forge of Vulcan had been thrown open.
Falseron beheld Orlando coming so furiously,
that he thought him a Lucifer who had burst
his chain, and was quite of another mind than
when he proposed to have him all to himself.
On the contrary, he recommended himself to
his gods ; and turning away begged for a more
auspicious season for revenge. But Orlando
hailed and arrested him with a terrible voice,
saying, "O thou traitor! Was this the end to
which old quarrels were made up? Dost thou
not blush, thou and thy fellow-traitor Marsilius,
to have kissed me on the cheek like a Judas,
when last thou wert in France?"

Orlando had never shown such anger in his
countenance as he did that day. He dashed
at Falseron with a fury so swift, and at the
same time a mastery of his lance so marvellous,
that though he plunged it into the man's body
so as instantly to kill him, the body did not
move in the saddle. The hero himself, as he
rushed onward, was fain to see the end of a
stroke so perfect, and, turning his horse back,
he touched the carcass with his sword, and it

fell on the instant. They say, that it had no
soouer fallen than it disappeared. People got
off their horses to lift up the body, for it seemed
to be there still, the armor being left; but
when they came to handle the armor, it was
found as empty as the shell that is cast by a
lobster. O new, and strange, and portentous
event! proof manifest of the anger with which
God regards treachery.

When the first infidel army beheld their leader
dead, such fear fell upon them, that they were
for leaving the field to the Paladins; but they
were unable. Marsilius had drawn the rest of
his forces round the valley like a net, so that
their shoulders were turned in vain. Orlando
rode into the thick of them, with Count Anselm by his side. He rushed like a tempest;
and wherever he went, thunderbolts fell upon
helmets. The Paladins drove here and there
after them, each making a whirlwind round
about him and a bloody circle. Uliviero was
again in the *mêlée;* and Walter of Amulion
threw himself into it; and Baldwin roared like a
lion; and Avino and Avolio reaped the wretches'
heads like a turnip-field; and blows blinded
men's eyes; and Archbishop Turpin himself
had changed his crozier for a lance, and chased
a new flock before him to the mountains.

Yet what could be done against foes without

number? Multitudes fill up the spaces left by the dead without stopping. Marsilius, from his anxious and raging post, constantly pours them in. The Paladins are as units to thousands. Why tarry the horses of Rinaldo and Ricciardetto?

The horses did not tarry; but fate had been quicker than enchantment. Ashtaroth, nevertheless, had presented himself to Rinaldo in Egypt, as though he had issued out of a flash of lightning. After telling his mission, and giving orders to hundreds of invisible spirits round about him (for the air was full of them), he and Foul-Mouth, his servant, entered the horses of Rinaldo and Ricciardetto, which began to neigh and snort and leap with the fiends within them, till off they flew through the air over the pyramids, crowds of spirits going like a tempest before them. Ricciardetto shut his eyes at first, on perceiving himself so high in the air; but he speedily became used to it, though he looked down on the sun at last. In this manner they passed the desert, and the sea-coast, and the ocean, and swept the tops of the Pyrenees, Ashtaroth talking to them of wonders by the way; for he was one of the wisest of the devils, and knew a great many things which were then unknown to man. He laughed, for instance, as they went over sea, at the no-

tion, among other vain fancies, that nothing
was to be found beyond the pillars of Hercules ;
"for," said he, "the earth is round, and the
sea has an even surface all over ; and there are
nations on the other side of the globe, who
walk with their feet opposed to yours, and worship other gods than the Christians."

"Hah!" said Rinaldo ; "and may I ask
whether they can be saved?"

"It is a bold thing to ask," said the devil ;
"but do you take the Redeemer for a partisan,
and fancy He died for you only? Be assured He
died for the whole world, Antipodes and all.
Perhaps not one soul will be left out the pale of
salvation at last, but the whole human race
adore the truth, and find mercy. The Christian
is the only true religion ; but Heaven loves all
goodness that believes honestly, whatsoever the
belief may be."

Rinaldo was mightily taken with the humanity of the devil's opinions ; but they were now
approaching the end of their journey, and began to hear the noise of the battle ; and he
could no longer think of any thing but the delight of being near Orlando, and plunging into
the middle of it.

"You shall be in the very heart of it instantly," said his bearer. "I love you, and
would fain do all you desire. Do not fancy

that all nobleness of spirit is lost among us people below. You know what the proverb says, 'There's never a fruit, however degenerate, but will taste of its stock.' I was of a different order of beings once, and—— But it is well not to talk of happy times. Yonder is Marsilius; and there goes Orlando. Farewell, and give me a place in your memory."

Rinaldo could not find words to express his sense of the devil's good-will, nor that of Foul-Mouth himself. He said: "Ashtaroth, I am as sorry to part with you as if you were a brother; and I certainly do believe that nobleness of spirit exists, as you say, among your people below. I shall be glad to see you both sometimes, if you can come; and I pray God (if my poor prayer be worth any thing) that you may all repent and obtain His pardon; for without repentance, you know, nothing can be done for you."

"If I might suggest a favor," returned Ashtaroth, "since you are so good as to wish to do me one, persuade Malagigi to free me from his service, and I am yours for ever. To serve you will be a pleasure to me. You will only have to say, 'Ashtaroth,' and my good friend here will be with you in an instant."

"I am obliged to you," cried Rinaldo, "and so is my brother. I will write Malagigi, not

merely a letter, but a whole packetful of your
praises; and so I will to Orlando; and you shall
be set free, depend on it, your company has
been so perfectly agreeable."

"Your humble servant," said Ashtaroth, and
vanished with his companion like lightning.

But they did not go far.

There was a little chapel by the roadside in
Roncesvalles, which had a couple of bells; and
on the top of that chapel did the devils place
themselves, in order that they might catch the
souls of infidels as they died, and so carry them
off to the infernal regions. Guess if their
wings had plenty to do that day! Guess if
Minos and Rhadamanthus were busy, and
Charon sung in his boat, and Lucifer hugged
himself for joy. Guess, also, if the tables in
heaven groaned with nectar and ambrosia, and
good old St. Peter had a dry hair in his beard.

The two Paladins, on their horses, dropped
right into the middle of the Saracens, and began making such havoc about them, that Marsilius, who overlooked the fight from a mountain, thought his soldiers had turned one against
the other. He therefore descended in fury with
his third army; and Rinaldo, seeing him coming, said to Ricciardetto, "We had better be off
here, and join Orlando"; and with these words,
he gave his horse one turn round before he re-

treated, so as to enable his sword to make a
bloody circle about him; and stories say, that
he sheared off twenty heads in the twirl of it.
He then dashed through the astonished behold-
ers towards the battle of Orlando, who guessed
it could be no other than his cousin, and almost
dropped from his horse, out of desire to meet
him. Ricciardetto followed Rinaldo; and
Uliviero coming up at the same moment, the
rapture of the whole party is not to be expressed. They almost died for joy. After a
thousand embraces, and questions, and explana-
tions, and expressions of astonishment (for the
infidels held aloof awhile, to take breath from
the horror and mischief they had undergone),
Orlando refreshed his little band of heroes, and
then drew Rinaldo apart, and said: "O my
brother, I feel such delight at seeing you, I can
hardly persuade myself I am not dreaming.
Heaven be praised for it. I have no other wish
on earth, now that I see you before I die. Why
did n't you write? But never mind. Here you
are, and I shall not die for nothing."

"I did write," said Rinaldo, "and so did
Ricciardetto; but villainy intercepted our letters. Tell me what to do, my dear cousin; for
time presses, and all the world is upon us."

"Gan has brought us here," said Orlando,
"under pretence of receiving tribute from Mar-

silius—you see of what sort ; and Charles, poor
old man, is waiting to receive his homage at the
town of St. John ! I have never seen a lucky
day since you left us. I believe I have done for
Charles more than in duty bound, and that my
sins pursue me, and I and mine must all perish
in Roncesvalles."

"Look to Marsilius," exclaimed Rinaldo ;
"he is right upon us."

Marsilius was upon them, surely enough, at
once furious and frightened at the coming of
the new Paladins ; for his camp, numerous as
it was, had not only held aloof, but turned
about to fly like herds before the lion ; so he
was forced to drive them back, and bring up
his other troops, reasonably thinking that such
numbers must overwhelm at last, if they could
but be kept together.

Not the less, however, for this, did the Paladins continue to fight as if with joy. They killed
and trampled wheresoever they went ; Rinaldo
fatiguing himself with sending infinite numbers
of souls to Ashtaroth, and Orlando making a
bloody passage towards Marsilius, whom he
hoped to settle as he had done Falseron.

In the course of this his tremendous progress,
the hero struck a youth on the head, whose
helmet was so good as to resist the blow, but at
the same time flew off ; and Orlando seized him

by the hair to kill him. "Hold!" cried the
youth, as loud as want of breath could let him;
"you loved my father—I 'm Bujaforte."

The Paladin had never seen Bujaforte; but
he saw the likeness to the good old Man of the
Mountain, his father; and he let go the youth's
hair, and embraced and kissed him. "O Bujaforte!" said he; "I loved him indeed—my good
old man; but what does his son do here, fighting against his friend?"

Bujaforte was a long time before he could
speak for weeping. At length he said: "Orlando, let not your noble heart be pained with
ill thoughts of my father's son. I am forced to
be here by my lord and master Marsilius. I had
no friend left me in the world, and he took me
into his court, and has brought me here before
I knew what it was for; and I have made a show
of fighting, but have not hurt a single Christian.
Treachery is on every side of you. Baldwin
himself has a vest given him by Marsilius, that
every body may know the son of his friend
Gan, and do him no injury. See there—look
how the lances avoid him."

"Put your helmet on again," said Orlando,
"and behave just as you have done. Never will
your father's friend be an enemy to the son.
Only take care not to come across Rinaldo."

The hero then turned in fury to look for

Baldwin, who was hastening towards him at that moment with friendliness in his looks.

"'T is strange," said Baldwin; "I have done my duty as well as I could, yet nobody will come against me. I have slain right and left, and cannot comprehend what it is that makes the stoutest infidels avoid me."

"Take off your vest," cried Orlando, contemptuously, "and you will soon discover the secret, if you wish to know it. Your father has sold us to Marsilius, all but his honorable son."

"If my father," cried Baldwin, impetuously tearing off the vest, "has been such a villain, and I escape dying any longer, by God! I will plunge this sword through his heart. But I am no traitor, Orlando; and you do me wrong to say it. You do me foul dishonor, and I 'll not survive it. Never more shall you behold me alive."

Baldwin spurred off into the fight, not waiting to hear another word from Orlando, but constantly crying out, "You have done me dishonor"; and Orlando was very sorry for what he had said, for he perceived that the youth was in despair.

And now the fight raged beyond all it had done before; and the Paladins themselves began to fall, the enemy were driven forward in such multitudes by Marsilius. There was unhorsing of foes, and reseating of friends, and great cries, and anguish, and unceasing labor; and twenty Pagans went down for one Christian; but still the Christians fell. One Paladin disappeared after another, having too much to do for mortal men. Some could not make way through the press for very fatigue of killing, and others were hampered with the falling horses and men. Sansonetto was thus beaten to earth by the club of Grandonio; and Walter d'Amulion had his shoulders broken; and Angiolin of Bayona, having lost his lance, was thrust down by Marsilius, and Angiolin of Bellonda by Sirionne; and Berlinghieri and Ottone are gone; and then Astolfo went, in revenge of whose death Orlando turned the spot on which he died into a gulf of Saracen blood. Rinaldo met the luckless Bujaforte, who had just begun to explain how he seemed to be fighting on the side which his father hated, when the impatient hero exclaimed, "He who is not with me is against me"; and gave him a volley of such horrible cuffs about the head and ears, that Bujaforte died without being able to speak another word. Orlando, cutting his way to a spot in which there was a great struggle and uproar, found the poor youth Baldwin, the son of Gan, with two spears in his breast. "I am no traitor now," said Baldwin; and so saying, fell dead to the earth ; and Orlando lifted up his voice and wept, for he was bitterly sorry to have been the cause of his death. He then joined Rinaldo in the hottest of the tumult ; and all the surviving Paladins gathered about them, including Turpin the archbishop, who fought as hardily as the rest ; and the slaughter was lavish and horrible, so that the eddies of the wind chucked the blood into the air, and earth appeared a very seething cauldron of hell. At length down went Uliviero himself. He had become blind with his own blood, and smitten Orlando without knowing him, who had never received such a blow in his life.

"How now, cousin !" cried Orlando; "have you too gone over to the enemy ?"

"O my lord and master, Orlando," cried the other, " I ask your pardon, if I have struck you. I can see nothing—I am dying. The traitor Arcaliffe has stabbed me in the back ; but I killed him for it. If you love me, lead my horse into the thick of them, so that I may not die unavenged."

"I shall die myself before long," said Orlando, "out of very toil and grief; so we will go together. I have lost all hope, all pride, all wish to live any longer : but not my love for Uliviero. Come—let us give them a few blows yet ; let them see what you can do with your dying hauds.   One faith, one death, one only wish be ours.''

Orlando led his cousin's horse where the press was thickest, and dreadful was the strength of the dying man and of his half-dying companion.   They made a street, through which they passed out of the battle ; and Orlando led his cousin away to his tent, and said : '' Wait a little till I return, for I will go and sound the horn on the hill yonder.''

'' 'T is of no use,'' said Uliviero ; '' and my spirit is fast going, and desires to be with its Lord and Saviour.''   He would have said more, but his words came from him imperfectly, like those of a man in a dream ; only his cousin gathered that he meant to commend to him his sister, Orlando's wife, Alda the Fair, of whom indeed the great Paladin had not thought so much in this world as he might have done. And with these imperfect words he expired.

But Orlando no sooner saw him dead than he felt as if he was left alone on the earth ; and he was quite willing to leave it ; only he wished that Charles at St. John Pied de Port should hear how the case stood before he went ; and so he took up the horn, and blew it three times with such force that the blood burst out of his nose and mouth.   Turpin says that at the third blast the horn broke in two.

In spite of all the noise of the battle the sound of the horn broke over it like a voice out of the other world. They say that birds fell dead at it, and that the whole Saracen army drew back in terror. But fearfuller still was its effect at St. John Pied de Port. Charlemagne was sitting in the midst of his court when the sound reached him ; and Gan was there. The emperor was the first to hear it.

"Did you hear that?" said he to his nobles. "Did you hear the horn as I heard it?"

Upon this they all listened ; and Gan felt his heart misgive him.

The horn sounded the second time.

"What is the meaning of this?" said Charles.

"Orlando is hunting," observed Gan, "and the stag is killed. He is at the old pastime that he was so fond of in Aspramonte."

But when the horn sounded yet a third time, and the blast was one of so dreadful a vehemence, everybody looked at the other, and then they all looked at Gan in fury. Charles rose from his seat. "This is no hunting of the stag," said he. "The sound goes to my very heart, and, I confess, makes me tremble. I am awakened out of a great dream. O Gan! O Gan! Not for thee do I blush, but for myself, and for nobody else. O my God, what is to be done! But whatever is to be done must be done quickly. Take this villain, gentlemen, and keep him in hard prison. O foul and monstrous villain! Would to God I had not lived to see this day! O obstinate and enormous folly! O Malagigi, had I but believed thy foresight! 'T is thou wert the wise man, and I the gray-headed fool."

Ogier the Dane, and Namo and others, in the bitterness of their grief and anger, could not help reminding the emperor of all which they had foretold. But it was no time for words. They put the traitor into prison; and then Charles, with all his court, took his way to Roncesvalles, grieving and praying.

It was afternoon when the horn sounded, and half an hour after it when the emperor set out; and meantime Orlando had returned to the fight that he might do his duty, however hopeless, as long as he could sit his horse, and the Paladins were now reduced to four; and though the Saracens suffered themselves to be mowed down like grass by them and their little band, he found his end approaching for toil and fever, and so at length he withdrew out of the fight, and rode all alone to a fountain which he knew of, where he had before quenched his thirst.

His horse was wearier still than he, and no sooner had its master alighted, than the beast, kneeling down as if to take leave, and to say, "I have brought you to your place of rest," fell dead at his feet. Orlando cast water on him from the fountain, not wishing to believe him dead; but when he found it to no purpose he grieved for him as if he had been a human being, and addressed him by name in tears, and asked forgiveness if ever he had done him wrong. They say that the horse, at these words, once more opened his eyes a little, and looked kindly at his master, and so stirred never more.

They say also that Orlando then, summoning all his strength, smote a rock near him with his beautiful sword Durlindana, thinking to shiver the steel in pieces, and so prevent its falling into the hands of the enemy ; but though the rock split like a slate, and a deep fissure remained ever after to astonish the eyes of pilgrims, the sword remained unhurt.

"O strong Durlindana," cried he, "O noble and worthy sword, had I known thee from the first as I know thee now, never would I have been brought to this pass."

And now Rinaldo and Ricciardetto and Turpin came up, having given chase to the Saracens till they were weary, and Orlando gave joyful welcome to his cousin, and they told him how the battle was won, and then Orlando knelt before Turpin, his face all in tears, and begged remission of his sins, and confessed them, and Turpin gave him absolution ; and suddenly a light came down upon him from heaven like a rainbow, accompanied with a sound of music, and an angel stood in the air blessing him, and then disappeared ; upon which Orlando fixed his eyes on the hilt of his sword as on a crucifix, and embraced it and said : "Lord, vouchsafe that I may look on this poor instrument as on the symbol of the tree upon which Thou sufferedst Thy unspeakable martyrdom !" and so adjusting the sword to his bosom, and embracing it closer, he raised his eyes, and appeared like a creature seraphical and transfigured ; and in bowing his head he breathed out his pure soul. A thunder was then heard in the heavens, and the heavens opened and seemed to stoop to the earth, and a flock of angels was seen like a white cloud ascending with his spirit, who were known to be what they were by the trembling of their wings. The white cloud shot out golden fires, so that the whole air was full of them ; and the voices of the angels mingled in song with the instruments of their brethren above, which made an inexpressible harmony, at once deep and dulcet. The priestly warrior Turpin, and the two Paladins, and the hero's squire Terigi, who were all on their knees, forgot their own beings, in following the miracle with their eyes.

It was now the office of that squire to take horse and ride off to the emperor at St. John Pied de Port, and tell him of all that had occurred; but in spite of what he had just seen, he lay for a time overwhelmed with grief. He then rose, and mounted his steed, and left the Paladins and the archbishop with the dead body, who knelt about it, guarding it with a weeping love.

The good squire Terigi met the emperor and his cavalcade coming towards Roncesvalles, and alighted and fell on his knees, telling him the miserable news, and how all his people were slain but two of his Paladins, and himself, and the good archbishop. Charles for anguish began tearing his white locks; but Terigi comforted him against so doing, by giving an account of the manner of Orlando's death, and how he had surely gone to heaven. Nevertheless, the squire himself was broken-hearted with grief and toil; and he had scarcely added a denouncement of the traitor Gan, and a hope that the emperor would appease Heaven finally by giving his body to the winds, than he said: "The cold of death is upon me"; and so he fell dead at the emperor's feet.

Charles was ready to drop from his saddle for

wretchedness. He cried out : "Let nobody comfort me more. I will have no comfort. Cursed be Gan, and cursed this horrible day, and this place, and every thing. Let us go on, like blind miserable men that we are, into Roncesvalles ; and have patience if we can, out of pure misery, like Job, till we do all that can be done."

So Charles rode on with his nobles ; and they say that for the sake of the champion of Christendom and the martyrs that died with him, the sun stood still in the sky till the emperor had seen Orlando, and till the dead were buried.

Horrible to his eyes was the sight of the field of Roncesvalles. The Saracens, indeed, had forsaken it, conquered ; but all his Paladins but two were left on it dead ; and the slaughtered heaps among which they lay made the whole valley like a great dumb slaughter-house, trampled up into blood and dirt, and reeking to the heat. The very trees were dropping with blood ; and every thing, so to speak, seemed tired out, and gone to a horrible sleep.

Charles trembled to his heart's core for wonder and agony. After dumbly gazing on the place, he again cursed it with a solemn curse, and wished that never grass might grow within it again, nor seed of any kind, neither within it nor on any of its mountains around with their proud shoulders; but the anger of Heaven abide over it forever, as on a pit made by hell upon earth.

Then he rode on, and came up to where the body of Orlando awaited him with the Paladins, and the old man, weeping, threw himself as if he had been a reckless youth from his horse, and embraced and kissed the dead body, and said: "I bless thee, Orlando. I bless thy whole life, and all that thou wast; and all that thou ever didst, and thy mighty and holy valor, and the father that begot thee; and I ask pardon of thee for believing those who brought thee to thine end. They shall have their reward, O thou beloved one! But, indeed, it is thou that livest, and I that am worse than dead."

And now, behold a wonder. For the emperor, in the fervor of his heart and of the memory of what had passed between them, called to mind that Orlando had promised to give him his sword, should he die before him; and he lifted up his voice more bravely, and adjured him even now to return it to him gladly; and it pleased God that the dead body of Orlando should rise on its feet, and kneel as he was wont to do at the feet of his liege lord, and gladly, and with a smile on its face, return the sword to the Emperor Charles. As Orlando rose, the

Paladins and Turpin knelt down out of fear and horror, especially seeing him look with a stern countenance; but when they saw that he knelt also, and smiled, and returned the sword, their hearts became reassured, and Charles took the sword like his liege lord, though trembling with wonder and affection : and in truth he could hardly clench his fingers around it.

Orlando was buried in a great sepulchre in Aquisgrana, and the dead Paladins were all embalmed and sent with majestic cavalcades to their respective counties and principalities, and every Christian was honorably and reverently put in the earth, and recorded among the martyrs of the Church.

But meantime the flying Saracens, thinking to bury their own dead, and ignorant of what still awaited them, came back into the valley, and Rinaldo beheld them with a dreadful joy, and showed them to Charles. Now the emperor's cavalcade had increased at every moment; and they fell upon the Saracens with a new and unexpected battle, and the old emperor, addressing the sword of Orlando, exclaimed : "My strength is little, but do thou do thy duty to thy master, thou famous sword, seeing that he returned it to me smiling, and that his revenge is in my hands." And so saying, he met Balugante, the leader of the infidels, as he came borne along by his frightened horse; and the old man, raising the sword with both hands, cleaved him, with a delighted mind, to the chin.

O sacred Emperor Charles! O well-lived old man! Defender of the Faith! light and glory of the old time! thou hast cut off the other ear of Malchus, and shown how rightly thou wert born into the world, to save it a second time from the abyss.

Again fled the Saracens, never to come to Christendom more: but Charles went after them into Spain, he and Rinaldo and Ricciardetto and the good Turpin; and they took and fired Saragossa; and Marsilius was hung to the carob-tree under which he had planned his villainy with Gan; and Gan was hung, and drawn and quartered, in Roncesvalles, amidst the execrations of the country.

And if you ask, how it happened that Charles ever put faith in such a wretch, I shall tell you that it was because the good old emperor, with all his faults, was a divine man, and believed in others out of the excellence of his own heart and truth. And such was the case with Orlando himself.

THE END